WE, 1

BY EDWARD J. INDOVINA

Published by Starry Night Publishing.Com
Rochester, New York

Edward J. Indovina

Contents

Edward J. Indovina

<u>**Dedication:**</u>

This work is dedicated to my Mother and Father. Without whose sacrifices and love I would have never had the great childhood that I had. Of which, in turn, gave me the inspiration and the mettle to not only attempt, but to complete this work.

Also, and not least: My Grandfather Serafin Gayo-Arias, whose courage and tenacity made all of this possible.

Edward J. Indovina

<u>Preface</u>

First, allow me to preface this essay (it is a preface after all), by saying that this is a book of fiction. While many of the characters and incidents are based upon actual people, the framework of the novel is purely fictional.

Why do I emphasize this? Because while some writers are able to write historical novels based upon people from written history or interviews with the subject, unfortunately, I was not able to. Serafin had passed away before I was born. Therefore, the background material that I had at my disposal was either the actual immigration records, a copy of his passport that my Mother, his daughter, had, or the spoken stories of what he was like.

Was this a detriment to creating this version of his story?

No. Absolutely not.

I have always had a fascination/curiosity about the life of my grandfather, Serafin. On the one hand, I saw an extraordinary legacy that he left behind. Three daughters, who, in turn, had good husbands and, they, in turn, raised productive, responsible children. Now, mind you, it wasn't just four or five children. No, in total between the three of them there is a grand total of sixteen of Serafin's direct grandchildren and not one of them (besides me, of course) is an unsavory character in the fabric of society. That, in and of itself, is a testament to the values and love that were provided by Serafin and Petrina, his wife and our Grandmother.

Now, don't misconstrue me, it is an absolute testimony to the parents that we sixteen brood had, why we are all, for the most part, functional. But, as everyone knows, if the foundation is solid then it is much easier to build additional layers that will be strong on top of it.

On the other hand, due to my, let's call it, 'curiosity for what life had to provide', there were numerous times when I would get disciplined by my mother with a recurrent statement of being 'just like her Father.' It got to be that sometimes she would simply give up and just call me Serafin instead of the name that she gave me. I actually grew proud to be called such, because I knew, regardless of how mad she would be at me, she loved her Father completely which also meant that she loved me enough to compare me to him.

But, I digress…

When I was first asked to construct a novel, my Professor asked me to write a modern day story in relation to the difficulties that are experienced by the working class in today's environment in the United States. While I had (have) my own strong opinions regarding the current political climate, I wanted this story to be different than the usual government bashing stories that seem to be in infinitesimal abundance now a days. After some thought it hit me. I could make this story, instead of a negative slam (which is terribly easy to do) against what we all perceive to be decreased opportunities in this country, into a tale showing how one man, in spite of the odds against him, created his own kingdom, in a land in which he adopted. Then, this man's life, in turn, inspires one of his progeny, to forge a new path in a similarly challenged time.

Does it work? I don't know. I am not the one to judge as such. You, the reader can make that determination. I will tell you this; that writing this book proved to be a catharsis and education of sorts for me. While I thought that I had a firmly perceived comprehension on what my Grandfather went through, it wasn't until I started digging into the recorded facts of his time period that I truly began to understand just how many barriers he had to overcome to raise his family.

First, and foremost, I truly learned that time does indeed repeat itself. If you look at the economic climate of Europe and the attitude towards immigration in this country at the time of this writing, it is eerily similar to the climate and attitudes of the 1920's when Serafin came over here. Also, I couldn't imagine nowadays anyone actually pursuing a job that enables you to inhale unfiltered coal and rail dust and working as hard as he did. And, that doesn't even begin to scratch the surface on the prejudices that were leveled against a Spanish man in a mixed marriage. It is no wonder, years later, when I would explore his work bench, that I found a pair of brass knuckles and a blackjack in addition to his various hand tools.

That being said, thank you for reading at least this far. I hope, if anything ,that this work will give some of you a little appreciation for the accomplishments to those that came before us and the obstacles that they overcame to achieve their quests.

Additionally, perhaps it will inspire some of us to stop looking for what's wrong and to look to what's right about this country and the great things that one can still achieve here.

Edward J. Indovina   March 25, 2013.

Edward J. Indovina

Chapter 1

"Forget the former things; do not dwell on the past.
See, I am doing a new thing!
Now it springs up; do you not perceive it?
I am making a way in the desert
and streams in the wasteland."
      Isaiah 43:18-19

"Sari. Must you go?" His mother's voice wavered in anticipation as she asked her loaded question, full knowing the reply from her youngest son.

"Madre, Si." He paused a moment before he answered, keeping his back towards his mother so he wouldn't have to see her face. "I must"

She stared out across the water, avoiding her son's eyes not wanting him to see the pain that was clearly shown on her face. "But why? Are you not happy here? Is there anything that I did to cause you distress?"

Serafin inhaled deeply before he answered. He didn't want to hurt his mother, it was the last thing on his mind. "Madre, it is not you. It's just... I don't feel that there is anything here for me."

"But what? What else do you want? Your brothers are content here. They have begun to make adult lives for themselves."

"That's just it Madre. I don't want to be just content. I don't want to have to make a life here. I just feel that there is more, much more, out there for me."

Serafin's mother started to become agitated. "Look at this land. How can you leave this? This, Regalo de Dios para nosotros. There is nothing in America that is like this!" she motioned towards the water with a grand gesture of her hands.

Isabella had a point. Where they stood was a portion of the magnificence of San Tome in Spain. The water, as it abutted to the land, was as if it was beauty personified. As the sun reflected off of the top of the water creating an illusory blue, mirror like surface that radiated it was as though you were in a heavenly aura.

In the urban area of the Puerto de Cambados, the fine white sands and the calm waters were almost physical embodiments of serenity. It was if the land's namesake, Saint Thomas himself, had blessed the land.

The land, with its attachment to the sea was the ultimate beautiful paradox. Soil and water that gave and provided also created an abhorrent danger by the work that they required by inhabitants to provide for them. Analogously they were similar in nature to St. Thomas, the apostle who had doubted Christ's resurrection, and yet, despite his grave indiscretion, was the only one who was deemed worthy to witness the assumption of our savior's beloved Mother Mary into Heaven's great embrace.

Isabella looked downward at the expansive green expanse and shook her head. Her long black and grey streaked hair reflecting in the sunlight.

"Sari, I understand how a young man feels. But... are you sure this is wise?"

Serafin took a seat on the lawn, looked up into his mother's eyes with his expressive hazel eyes and motioned for his mother to sit down beside him.

Isabella was a proud and strong woman. She was slight in stature, with a build similar to her fellow countrywomen. Born and raised in San Tome she didn't know anything beyond her immediate home. Not that this was a detrimental trait.

Like the majority of Spanish, or actually, European women of the time, she was expected to keep the home proper and ready for her family. Married young, she gave birth to three fine boys. While the work and trials of taking care of a husband and children were hard enough, she at times wearied from her work. Yet, she never ceased to let anything keep her from performing her duties. She never abjured to work hard or without tenacity.

However, it wasn't perceived as work. Assisting her husband tend the oxen, sow the crops, till the fields, and reap the yield was expected, not asked. After all, they were a team, not just husband and wife. For the Lord blessed and took after a worker, not an idler or bemoaner.

While she maintained her youthful beauty, the lines on her face betrayed her actual age. Every slight indentation and fold hid a story in and of itself. The strain of childbirth, the failure of the crops in '98, the loss of her parents, the flood of '01, the lean years, the miscarriage of her second child, and then the loss of her husband, Ramiel, Serafin's father were borne upon her face like a topographical map of life.

In the beginning, there is a deniability of mortality that comes along with marriage and raising a family. The daily responsibilities of a familial unit steamroll over any personal or inconsequential duties, that happens to manifest themselves to the married partners. The support of the brood through monetary, social, and spiritual material takes precedence over any personal desires. Making sure the children are comfortable and secure becomes the primary goal. In actuality, the last thing on a parent's mind is the thought of losing their partner or planning for such an occurrence.

The passing of her husband, Ramiel, unfortunately, placed Isabella into a different existence. Gone was her spouse and stronger half. Now, she was placed in the position of supporting and providing for her family on her own. While it would have been just as easy to surrender to the new burden, Isabella quietly took up the challenge. There was no time for self-pity. The Lord had deemed her strong enough for this challenge therefore she would embrace it, not mourn the plight that had befallen her.

In the beginning, she struggled to maintain the farm by herself or with the help of neighbors. She strained to maintain the integrity of the operation that she and her husband had established.

Unfortunately and ultimately, this proved to be a futile task. Yet, out of this, the one thing Isabella did discover, much to her chagrin was the self-interest that the majority of people maintained. When personal necessities arrived, the very people who assured her of aide chose to renege on their promises and tend to their own needs. Self-preservation was a more powerful motivator than a sense of charity among the people that she had hoped to assist her through her plight.

Isabella was at a crossroads now. Without the income from the farm, it would become difficult to care for her children. She could sell the farm but that would deprive her children of a real home.

Ramiel and she worked hard to procure the farm and its surrounding land. To surrender it now, after all of their hard work, would feel as though she folded under the grief and tragedy of losing her husband. While she thought of it, and so desperately wanted to envelop herself in self-consuming grief, she knew she could not succumb. No. That was not the way to raise her children. To allow her children to witness acquiescence and cowardice, was to show them a path of failure. That was a path, if shown, that they would surely follow when they acquired resistance and failure in their lifetimes. Children are led by examples, good and bad, she understood. Therefore, if the examples the children are brought up around are wrought with easy outs, then surely that is the path they will be more apt to take. "No hay honor en un cobarde" her padre used to say to her.

Isabella resigned herself to a decision. While she truly felt as though the Lord had abandoned her, she realized that she was also blessed in the same turn. Besides being a good wife and mother, the other gifts that the Lord gave her was an aptness and creativity with her hands. From the earliest days of her life Isabella found that she had a way with the needle and thread. Although she had no formal teaching in the art, she had naturally picked up the tools while watching her mother use them. Eventually, Isabella had become so adept at them that the entire family went to her instead of her mother for mending or creation of their clothes.

After Isabella's recognition of her current position in life she took it upon herself to create her own sewing, tailoring, and mending business. She often walked miles a day to the town and solicited business. In the beginning, it sometimes looked hopeless and she would walk home with no work in hand, but she soldiered on.

Eventually, the townsfolk would wait for her on Wednesdays when she would bring her clients' clothes and pick up more. Isabella, while first being known as the woman with three boys in tow, had also become known as the finest seamstress in the area and the well-to-do residents would entrust only her for their clothing alteration and mending needs. With her tenaciously hard work, Isabella was able to keep the farm and supply her family the means to survive.

Isabella broke free of her mind's wandering and took a seat next to her son and continued with her pleading. "Sari, you are so smart. Smarter even than your brothers. Why, you could eventually become Bishop or even Pope!"

Serafin shook his head as he rested his arms on his knees. "Madre, no. While I appreciate your beautiful words, I don't want that, or anything else here. At least, right now. It just doesn't seem to be a good place for a young man as myself here." Serafin avoided his mother's eyes as he finished his statement.

The problem, in Serafin's eyes, was that Spain in 1920 wasn't the most conducive of environments for a young man, or, any able bodied man, period. Spain, like the rest of the world at this time, was in a deep recession. The world financial markets were in dire straits and country after country was pulling back on services and assistance. In response to the dire economic conditions, many of Spain's fellow European countries were experiencing increased citizen protesting. Jobs and resources were scarce and the inhabitants were getting restless. People were expecting more from their leaders and their leaders weren't reciprocating in kind.

Spain, however, was hit worse than most countries. The Spain of 1920 had become a desolate country. The apathy and disregard to social growth on the behalf of the political leaders began to show the results of prior years of neglect. Spain's poor technological advancements contributed to a poor agricultural output which, in itself, led to very few economic opportunities. In addition, lending opportunities were relegated to the already well-to-do leaving the basic citizens nothing.

There was no opportunity for a man of meager means to obtain a loan in which to build a business. Of course, the fact that the Bank of Spain was privately owned didn't help matters, and it certainly didn't help the citizens of Spain.

In response to the failed economic conditions, the state turned to defense, order and justice to maintain control. The lethal combination of a poor economy and increased governmental and military power and control contributed to the growing discontentment of the working class.

Leanings towards social unrest and a push for socialism began to occupy the thoughts and actions of the working class. However, instead of listening to the people, some in higher places chose to take advantage of the unrest in the country for their own personal gain.

As the protests and strikes escalated, Spain was nearing the brink of a civil war, so, elitists such as General Primo de Rivera were beginning to place themselves in positions of more power. They learned that it was easy to take advantage of the failure of the prior ruling class to set themselves up for personal gain. By 1923, Rivera would lead a coup to establish a dictatorship of Spain. In the present time, though, the Spanish Foreign Legion was growing and recruiting more disenchanted and desperate young men into the ever darkening environment.

Serafin took a deep breath once again. "Madre, you know I love you, I love this country, but... I am young, I have an opportunity to see if I can make a better start. A new start…"

"But, America? Sari, they don't want us there."

"Perhaps they don't want some, but they will want me. It has to be better than the prospects here." Serafin reached over and gave his mother an embrace.

Isabella was right, though. By the early 1920s fewer and fewer Spaniards were emigrating to the United States. It would eventually turn out that in 1922 only 131 Spaniards would emigrate to America. In fact, ultimately, more Spaniards would actually leave the United States than enter it, choosing instead, other countries to emigrate to.

Isabella rose and took her son's hands as she consigned herself to the impending farewell. "Sari, perhaps you are right. You are a strong young man and I cannot tell you what to do. I am proud, very proud of the young man you have become."

Serafin looked up into his mother's eyes. "No, Madre. It is I who am honored to have a mother like you. You are the reason I am who I am. Your sacrifices and firmness have helped to develop me into who I am. However, I succeed or fail on my own. It is time."

Tears welled in Isabella's eyes. "Si, Sari. It is time. But, you cannot envidiar me for mi egoismo. After all, you are my last son."

"Te quiero, Madre. Te quiero." Tears streamed down Serafin's face as he gazed at his mother.

Serafin slept uneasily that night. He had packed his clothing into a single suitcase and fell wearily upon the bed. He excitedly thought about leaving his native Spain for America, yet was filled with the tinges of fear and trepidation that often accompanied decisions of this magnitude. What if it didn't work out like he thought? What if Madre was right, what if they didn't want him.

Then what? Run home with his tail between his legs? Well, in reality he probably couldn't. This trip was going to cost him nearly all of his savings. If he failed, he wouldn't have the luxury of returning. No, he mused, enough of these thoughts. He would make it. He would succeed. After all, he was brought up properly and he was a good person. He didn't shirk his duties or cause harm to others. The Lord would look after him as long as he worked hard and didn't forget his roots.

Before the roosters' crows had the opportunity to wake him, Serafin woke with a start. As the sun's rays came through the window and touched his face, he awoke. This was it, he had to take the train to the port and board the ship. As he quickly dressed he heard a noise from the kitchen.

Serafin peered from around the hallway into the kitchen.

"Madre, is that you?" he asked before he entered. The smell of the coffee brewing was a dead giveaway however.

"Si, it is I, your Madre," she answered standing before the stove, not turning around, preparing a meal of torriajas for her son.

"Did you not sleep, Madre?"

"Eh... I slept enough." Isabella answered.

Serafin looked at his mother adoringly. "Madre, I did not mean to interrupt your rest."

"What makes you think that it was you that it was you, un engreido?" Isabella turned from the stove and smiled at Serafin.

"I see, Madre. Are you going to eat all of that by yourself?"

"Sentarse, Sari. Sentarse! Did you think that I would let you leave on an empty stomach?"

Serafin sat down and adjusted himself. "No, no I didn't. But..."

"Shush, Sari. Sit and eat with me." Isabella plated the food and brought it to the table. "Now, you and I need to come to an understanding, my Sari."

Serafin started eating and looked at his mother. "What? What do you wish, mi reina."

"While I pray to the Lord to watch over you, know this. You will encounter good times and you will endure bad times. This, you must understand. However, the important thing is to never let either extreme defeat you. Never waver from the quest you choose. Remember, success and failure are merely two sides of the same coin. Neither of them last for long, No hay mal (ni bien) que cien anos dure. If you are good in heart, honest, and true to your maker, and you work hard, good things will come. As hard or as easy as things become, remember, nothing is achieved without hard work. Recall what your Padre would say to you; No hay miel sin hiel."

Serafin took a deep breath and reached across from the table to hold his mother's hands. "Si, entiendo, Madre. But, rest easy. I will work hard and I will not waver. I was taught by yours and Padre's example. Never once did you allow the hardships we endured keep you from providing for us."

Isabella smiled weakly and stood up. "One more thing, Sari"

"Yes?"

Isabella stared with a stern look at her son. Serafin braced himself for what was to possibly come.

"If you do not remember to write to me and let me know how you are doing I will be forced to travel to America to punish you!"

Isabella smiled broadly as she delivered her warning. The two of them laughed hard and long. Then both turned slightly somber as Serafin reached for his hat, coat, and suitcase. He paused before reaching for the articles. All three had belonged to his father. Now, by virtue of a similar build they were his. He couldn't help but feel proud of the fact that he was wearing his Father's hat and coat and that he was continuing their lives.

Mother and son looked at each other. No additional words needed to be said. Serafin kissed his mother on the forehead and Isabella turned to the sink to wash the dishes. Serafin took one last look as he exited out the door to make his way to the seaport.

As Serafin walked up the dirt road he proceeded to hitch a ride on Senor Alvares' wagon for the trip to the port.

When Serafin arrived at the port it was intimidating. To a young man who had only known the open fields and serene waters of his home it was a little daunting. The ships appeared enormous and the hustle of the passengers and workers was something that Serafin hadn't seen before.

The port was crowded but not terribly so. Serafin made his way down the center of the port Serafin looked up towards the ship docked there. To a young man from a small town in Spain the ship looked enormous. The Niagara, as it was named, was fifty-eight feet wide and four-hundred-forty feet long. She was built in 1908 and was beginning to belie her age.

Originally a tanker ship, the Niagara was built by Flensburger Schiffsbau Geselleschaft in Flensburg Germany. She was built as a tanker ship for Deutsch Amerik, Petroleum Ges. Eventually, after being sold a few times she was converted into a transport ship to take advantage of the emigration wave from Europe to America. After the conversion, profits were more lucrative than they were when she was a simple transport ship.

Serafin walked up the gangway and stepped onto the deck of the ship. Showing his ticket to the steward, Serafin was directed toward the lower decks. He had bought a ticket for the third class berth. Serafin, while he had toiled and saved, didn't feel that it was worth it to pay so much more to travel in first or even second class. Yes, the "steerage" passengers had meager to no accommodations. There was simply a bunk and a single washroom along with buckets in case of sickness. But, Serafin figured, it would only be a fortnight that he would have to endure before he reached America. To suffer slightly, the rewards to follow would be great. At least that was what he hoped. After all, he said to himself, Christ himself fell three times on his way to ascension to heaven.

Serafin made his way down the stairs of the ship towards the steerage area. The air began to become thick as he progressed down the stairs. There was little to no air flow in the bottom bowels of the ship. Smog, exhaust fumes, and the smell of human odor were the dominant emanations. Serafin felt dirty just descending the stairs even though the walls and floors had been hosed down just recently.

Serafin found his bunk, if one could call it that. Essentially it was a squared off area with a curtain in the front for privacy. A hammock was slung up from the corners for sleeping along with a chair and crate which would serve as a table.

The passage was long and tiring, and perceptually more than what it actually was. Serafin would be able to endure the conditions but others perhaps wouldn't be so strong. It was a known fact that some didn't survive the trip across the Atlantic in steerage. Many of the emigrants who traveled to America were not well originally when they boarded the ship. They blamed their maladies and misfortune on their surroundings of their native lands. The thought was, that a fresh start would afford them good fortune. Re-locating to America, the land of the free, could change their fate.

Serafin adjusted himself within his bunk. He would use this time, the days of travel, to rest and prepare himself for his journey ahead. To keep himself otherwise occupied he would read the translating books he brought with him and practice his English. The one thing that he did not want to do is enter a new country without knowing some of the language. He had heard too many stories of fellow immigrants being taken advantage of and ruined by unscrupulous individuals. And, while the government and employers of America were welcoming immigrants, many of the citizens were not so agreeable to the influx of new citizens. While they didn't want to take the jobs that only the immigrants were willing to do, there was this growing sentiment that the influx of immigrants were responsible for their lack of jobs and livelihood.

"Oh, yo no me siento muy bien"

Serafin's ears perked up. He heard the woman's voice from where he was down at the end of the steerage compartment.

"AAiieeee. No, No...Alguien la ayude!"

Serafin jumped up and ran down the hall until he encountered the source of the screaming.

There, in a cramped berth was a young girl and perhaps her older sister. The girl did not appear to be more than 16, and she was vomiting violently. Her sister had obtained a bucket but all that was serving to do was prevent the discharge from soiling the surrounding areas.

Serafin noticed the girl sweating profusely and shaking violently. While he was not a physician by any stretch of the imagination he recognized panic when he saw it. They had been on the ship for six days and there were only a few days left till their arrival in America. He knew if he didn't act fast she would not make it.

"Pardon, but I need to get you to the wash room."

The sister looked at Serafin with wide fearful eyes. "No! We do not know you! No, no te conozco!" she pushed Serafin away.

"Por favor, se tienen miedo! I know you are frightened but, please...confia en mi, you can trust me!"

Serafin looked at the sister with pleading eyes. She looked into his eyes deeply and concertedly. She answered him in measured tones watching him intently.

"Why? Why should we trust you? My sister is sick and all the steward wanted to do was grope me! El cerdo!"

Serafin had heard of this but he knew he had no time to waste on reasoning and empathizing with this woman. If he did not act quickly, the sick girl would be in grave danger.

"Suficiente! I am not the steward and you are not the sick one! Mi nombre es Serafin! We need to get her to the wash room now before she becomes gravely ill!"

The woman started to respond but one look at Serafin's determined eyes and a look at her sister, she chose to quell her thought.

"Bien, now what can you do for her?"

"Me ayudan!"

With that Serafin picked up the ill girl and instructed her sister to clear a path to the wash room. As they made their way down the hall heads peeked out of the berths to see the identity of the voice that they had heard moments earlier. Yet, for all their curiosity none of them were courageous enough to attempt to help her.

"Date prisa! Esta en etado de shock!" Serafin yelled to the woman.

"Patience! We are almost there!"

With that the woman threw open the worn curtain that was supposed to provide privacy for the inhabitants of the wash room and looked to Serafin for instructions.

"Turn on the water! Cold! Frio!"

The woman did as instructed and the water flowed from the shower head. Serafin quickly thrust the young girl under the stream of teeth chattering water.

"Usted esta matando!"

"No, I am bringing her out of her panic!"

As Serafin said this the woman noticed that where the initial shock of cold water on her sister had caused worse convulsions, eventually the impact of the water seemed to bring a calmness upon her. Now the girl had ceased convulsing and was merely shivering.

Serafin acted quickly to grab a towel and wrap it around the young girl as he pulled her out of the stream of water.

"Relajarse, Relajarse..." He said softly to the girl as she began to calm down. She calmed so much so that she almost fell into a sleep.

"Que hiciste? How did you know what to do?" Her sister asked incredulously as she moved quickly to snatch her sister protectively from Serafin's arms.

Serafin smiled slightly, "Mira, I may not know much, but I can recognize when someone is going into shock. I merely did what I had to do."

She looked at him suspiciously, "But why? What are your real motives?"

Serafin laughed out loud.

"I have no real motives save for looking out for someone suffering a misfortune. And, that it is what I merely did. Now, if you will excuse me, I will go back to my berth."

She looked Serafin up and down with extreme interest.

"Si, si. Gracias."

The young girl, wrapped in towels and blankets by now looked towards Serafin and said in a voice almost inaudible, "El Senor te ha puesto a su servicio."

The sister, as she guided her sibling to their berth looked at Serafin. "Mi nombre es Maria. Gracias..."

Serafin merely nodded.

With that, they made their way down the hall.

The rest of the trip went by relatively uneventful. Serafin rested in his berth counting the hours until the end of the trip.

"Atencion!, Atencion!" the Steerage steward bellowed. "We are arriving at port shortly. Everyone gather their belongings and wait for further instructions!"

Finally, the trip was over. And none too soon, thought Serafin. By now, the stench of the steerage deck was becoming almost unbearable. While they had amenities to maintain cleanliness it simply wasn't adequate. Many of the passengers in steerage simply took to maintaining a more relaxed attitude towards hygiene. In a sense, no one could blame them. While the upper decks contained upwards of four wash areas per thirty to forty passengers the steerage deck had only two for seven-hundred passengers. It didn't take a mathematician to figure out the problems that would arise with this set up.

In fact, it was safe to say that most of the passengers were relieved to know the end of the trip was near.

Of course, the announcement and subsequent docking of the ship didn't end their brief purgatory stay in steerage. The first class and second class passengers were allowed to depart the ship first. After a wait of an hour the steerage passengers were allowed to begin departure. Serafin began the climb up the stairs from the purgatory of steerage to the new air above.

The view was everything he had dreamed about and more. When Serafin reached the top deck of the Niagara he took a deep breath. The air helped to rejuvenate his senses from the sickening stench of human odors and waste of the lower deck where he traveled.

His eyes adjusted to the natural light slowly and then it appeared as a vision to him. She stood there in all of her majesty with torch raised and gleaming radiantly in the sunlight. Lady Liberty, herself a gift from a fellow European country, was there to welcome all to her shores, America, the land of legendary opportunity.

Edward J. Indovina

Chapter 2

Your offspring shall be like the dust of the earth, and you shall spread abroad to the west and to the east and to the north and to the south, and in you and your offspring shall all the families of the earth be blessed.
Genesis 28:14

"Remy, could you pick up Sari from school tonight? He has track practice and won't be getting out until at least 6." Rachiel was standing by the sink cleaning the morning dishes as everyone else was seated at the table.

The kitchen was a nice, modern kitchen typical of new builds. Granite countertops, deep-well sink and Kohler faucets were some of the nicer parts of the room. In the center was the ever-popular "island" where the family could eat casually, particularly breakfast and lunch. The island was surrounded by hi-top chairs.

Remy sighed audibly. "Yeah, I can do it, I guess." Sari looked at his father as his mother spoke with a typical teen-age smirk.
Sari was Rachiel and Remy's oldest. He was 15 years old and just beginning to display his adult features. Taller than his father at six feet, Sari had a similar build. Thin, yet muscular, his ectomorphic frame belied his strength. In fact, many of his school mates in phys-ed commented on his surprising power in various sporting activities.

"Well, can you or can't you? I have to take Angela to dance class and I know she won't be getting out until at least 6:15 or later. That teacher of hers thinks the sun rises and sets with her class. Heaven forbid some of the kids are just taking it for recreation, not a yenta career." She said tiredly.

The kids loved it when mom became sarcastic in tone towards the other adults in their lives. Rachiel always had a tough edge to her and they enjoyed that part of their mother.

Rachiel was slight in build and despite her advancing age was still attractive. Her raven hair did little to conceal her ethnic European origins, however.

Angela peered over her school books and looked over towards her father, waiting for his sassy retort, however, it didn't arrive with its usual zing.

Angela was the younger child of the family. At 14 years old she was similar in build to her mother yet contained many of her father's distinct features. Her nose was well sculpted and narrow, her eyes were large and hazel in color, and her hair was a mixture of black and dark brown. High arching eyebrows helped to highlight her facial features. She was going to be a very attractive woman in the years to come.

"Rach, yes, I'll make it." Remy emphasized his words in a blasé manner.

Rachiel looked over at her husband, smiling. "Yes, I know you will. Are you OK lately? You seem so pre-occupied, you don't seem to be yourself."

Remy shook his head knowingly.

"Huh, oh yeah, I'm fine honey. You know, just work and such. Why? Who do you want me to be? Fred Astaire?" He got up off his stool and slid across the faux hardwood floors in a pseudo dance move and then sat back down. Remy exposed his age with the statement. Few people, including his wife, knew who Astaire was anymore.

Rachiel let the quip and silliness go by her on purpose and continued her line of questioning. The children giggled amongst themselves.

"Why? What's going on at work? I just saw in the paper that your firm is in line for a federal grant. That's got to be exciting? Isn't it?"

Remy rolled his eyes. Obviously the news programs had picked up on his firm being one of the finalists for the government's "green" grants. These were grants that were being doled out to firms who developed and supported alternative energy sources. While it was all well and good, Remy couldn't help but feel it was merely grandstanding between his company and the current Presidential administration. He had yet to witness or hear of a viable, profitable, "green" energy program or company, for that matter, that wasn't heavily funded and backed by the federal government. And, he was in the business!

"Well, yeah, that's true but that will also mean a lot more work for those of us in support positions. This, of course, means they'll be introducing new systems, new regulations, and more paperwork for us to figure out without the proper training. You watch!"

Rachiel shook her head in disbelief and rolled her eyes. "So? What's the big deal? I've never seen you not figure out something that you've put your mind to"

Remy smirked and looked down, "thanks mom."

"You know what I mean Mr. Gayo! And, let me remind you, I am not your mother and never intend to be!" Rachiel commented firm but playfully.

Remy took another spoonful of his cereal and smirked. "Thank God! I don't think I could handle watching you do the ironing every Wednesday night with curlers in your hair!"

Angela and Sari started giggling with the image of their mother in such a pose.

"All right, enough of you guys! Let's move it!"

The children gathered their bowls and rushed them to the sink. As they deposited their utensils in the sink they gathered up their school materials and walking over the faux hardwood floors slipped into their shoes and proceeded to the front door.

Rachiel grabbed a towel and chased the kids to a hustle out while snapping the towel at their backsides. "Sari! Don't forget your math homework! Angie! Make sure you know your English work!" Rachiel yelled out after the quickly moving kids as they made their way down the paved driveway towards the front of the yard to wait for the arrival of the school bus.

Rachiel, having addressed the children turned her attention towards her husband, the biggest kid, in her opinion. "And you, Mr. Gayo. No more of this whining." She stabbed the air with her right index finger. " You know you can do it!"

Rachiel placed a well awaited kiss on Remy, who smiled and looked at his wife as he raised himself from the stool and gathered up his utensils to place in the sink.

Remy looked at his wife with a teasing yet wholly serious look and uttered: "What did I do to deserve you?"

"You convinced my Father to let me marry a Spaniard instead of an Italian! Now, go before your late!" Rachiel answered as Remy made his way to the foyer.

Remy turned to his wife once again. "How about you? Aren't you working today?"

"Yes, I am, dizzy. But I don't go in till 10 today"

"Nice life, Regina Rachiel!"

Rachiel looked down at the mess in the sink that she had to address before her day continued. "Tell you what, smart guy, you better move it or you're going to show up to work with my size 6 planted upside your head!"

Remy saluted his wife. "Yes'm miss Rachiel!"

Remy playfully hopped out the door towards his car, a late model Saturn L200 and left for work.

Chapter 3

As Serafin was ushered off of the Niagara he joined his fellow passengers in what was to become known as the Great Hall. Ellis Island was the portal where all immigrant hopefuls entered the United States. It was at this venue where the hopeful were deemed worthy to enter the United States. While there was a class system on the ocean liner, here on Ellis Island everyone was the same regardless of where you rode on the ship or the amount of income that you have. No amount of social connections or cash could reverse a disease or illness that would prevent them from being admitted into the United States. Although the Transatlantic companies tried to create a class system based upon their passengers' travel accommodations, the ever increasing turmoil within the United States prevented such. The growing anti-immigrant movement that was prevalent helped to ensure that any emigrant allowed into the United States would be disease free.

As the passengers climbed the stairs to the entrance of the Great Hall medical examiners watched the group closely from the top of the stairs. They took note of any passengers experiencing difficulty climbing the stairs and marked them for further examination. While Serafin climbed the steps he felt that same feeling of nervousness and excitement at the same time that he had before. The adrenalin was making him sweat, and he hoped that the medical examiners wouldn't mistake that for something else.

As Serafin followed the crowd, the passengers were then directed into the Medical Examining room. Anyone who was of questionable health was marked with a chalked 'X' on their backs. If they were deemed too ill to continue they were then admitted into the on-site hospital. Those that were unlucky enough to be determined to have contagious diseases were shipped back to their country of origin at the freight liner's expense.

Serafin, at this time, had also started to feel pangs of guilt. He began to realize what he had left behind in San Tome. His mother had wanted him to follow his brothers into the seminary but Serafin had other plans. "There has to be something more" he used to ponder to himself. Yes, being a priest was a noble and elevating position in Spanish society, but he just didn't feel it was for him.

And, likewise, staying in Spain to do anything else just wasn't an option. The winds of change were blowing in Spain and he didn't feel comfortable in his native land anymore. The Spanish Foreign Legion had begun to impart its influence, and, more importantly, Francisco Franco was in charge of it. Franco was a young, ambitious soldier that Serafin just did not get a good feeling from. It began to look to Serafin that if a young man didn't go into the priesthood or other untouchable profession that he had no choice but to go into the service of the legion in order to survive. Going to America, while it almost felt as if he was running away from his home and his family, was almost unthinkable. But, something in his gut told him that this is what he needed to do.

The medical examiners studied Serafin in their quick fashion. The exam would later become to be known as the "six second medical exam" It consisted of a quick look in the mouth, eyes, ears and skin color on the hands which served as the exam. Of course, at 5'7" and 160 pounds, Serafin was the picture of health. At seventeen years of age he was as hale and fit as any other young man who lived already in America.

After Serafin had passed the examination he was directed to the Registry room. As he entered the room he felt dwarfed by the sheer number of people that were in the room. The line snaked around in winding rows all leading to a man seated under a portrait of George Washington and an American flag to the right of the seated man. The man was elevated upon a platform and he appeared to Lord over the people that approached him. Suddenly, Serafin felt more uncomfortable here than he did in the Great Hall.

The wait was long. Serafin spent the times not moving and seated on his suitcase. He scanned the room to kill the boredom and before long he was aroused from his daydreaming when he heard his name called aloud.

"Serafin!" he recognized the voice but couldn't locate it. He looked around the room to search for its source.

"Serafin! Mi salvador y protector de mi sistere!"

Serafin turned around and finally located the voice. There, he saw her, Maria, sweet little Maria.

"Hola, Maria. It is good to see you! Como esta tu hermana?"

"Beuno, bueno. Lord be praised thanks to you!" She threw her arms around Serafin with a strong hug.

"Soy feliz! And... you are well?"

"Wonderful! Maravilloso! It is like nothing ever happened."

Maria looked into Serafin's eyes deeply.

"If.. If there is ever..." she paused embarrassedly. "Ever anything that you need. Do not hesitate to call on me. I will deliver. I..." tears filled her eyes. "I... we... owe you all. When no one else would help you appeared. Like your name, an angel...."

Serafin grabbed Maria's shoulder and turned her head towards his.

"Maria. Please, do not waste your prayers on me. I only did what anyone should do. What I was brought up to do. You were in need and I attempted to assist. This life we lead is hard enough. It should not be faced alone. If the Lord did not intend for us to help each other he would not have created so many of us."

Maria looked at him finally and wiped the welling tears from her eyes.

Serafin continued. "We are not alone. Nor, should we seek to be alone. We are placed on this earth with many different talents. Each of us are to complement the other. Our talents are God given and therefore should be used to aide one another. If we work together we can be a whole, as an individual, unfortunately, we are lacking. I merely lent my knowledge and experience to aid your sister in her plight. Alone, neither of us could have accomplished much, yet, together we rescued your sister!"

Maria smiled weakly. While she heard Serafin's words she did not feel them immediately. All she felt was an overwhelming debt of gratitude to this man, this good man, who helped when all others turned their heads.

Serafin then broke the silence. "Maria, you must go back to your place in line, otherwise you will be lost like a suckling pig who found his way to a fire pit!"

Maria turned and laughed. "You, you are a very interesting man. Dios los bendigna!"

She took Serafin's hand and kissed it. "Until the Lord deems that we shall meet again!"

She turned her back to Serafin and made her way back into the long line and Serafin smiled and re-seated himself on the suitcase.

<u>Chapter 4</u>

Remy arrived at his office at ten to nine. Walking through the front entrance he remembered that when he started at this job he used the rear entrance. He had worked for the firm for almost 20 years and throughout all of its incarnations. When he first joined them, their primary business was as an optics distribution firm. As the technologies changed in the country, so did the company's focus on its core products. In the 90's they began shifting their attention to digital camera applications and then, by the turn of the century, they started marketing imported, large lenses for solar panel applications.

The remodeling of the office made the company look like a large, international conglomerate which they were aiming to be. The exterior of the building had been transformed from the original concrete block look that it once had to a facade of decorative brick with faux pillars on either side of the entrance doors. In illuminated letters above the semi-circular awning was the company's name.

'SUNCOAST' displayed in large block letters served to announce to the surrounding businesses that they were in the midst of a great business entity. In a sense, it was as if the company was serving notice similar to what a well-dressed man that attends a casual luncheon portrays. "I can, therefore I will", in other words, don't adhere to the rules others set, forge your own way and ensure that you intimidate the others by projecting yourself above those rules and others.

As the company evolved, so did Remy and his duties within the company. When he started he was in distribution, or, more commonly know among the workers as a warehouse worker. Remy worked in that position for five years. As Remy displayed a dependable and competent work ethic he began to be recommended for more duties. This was the age where companies believed that the best employees were 'home grown'. Many companies subscribed to the credo that it was wiser to train and educate a promising employee to their own than inherit an employee that had another company's bad habits. Remy, fortunately was one that his supervisors recognized his increased aptitude and began shifting him into different departments. Remy went from truck loader, to dispatcher, into technical support, to his present job of sales coordinator.

With every change in job came more responsibility and more to learn. While Remy never finished college that didn't mean he wasn't smart. In fact, every job they assigned Remy he absorbed everything he could to make his job easier. Also, the company was quite generous in its employee training programs and Remy took advantage of every one he had to. However, personal gain didn't really motivate Remy. Remy was perfectly content to plan his time off as he was to plan time for his job. Remy just figured that with every job description change came an increased income and an opportunity to provide for his family. In addition, with every promotion came a new toy he could buy for his recreation activities.

Remy walked past the security station upon his entrance. The uniformed elderly man addressed Remy as he walked by. "Mornin' Rem. How're you this morning?"

Remy stopped mid stride and addressed the originator of the voice. He placed his elbow on the top of the security station and leaned in. "Good, Ben, good. How about yourself?"

"Hey, you know how it is. Did you see the game last night?

"Yeah, when are they going to win?"

"Yeah, same old Knicks. You know, I remember when they were good"

"When was that? When you were two? Don't show your age now Ben!" Remy laughed aloud and started off. Bem dismissed Remy with a wave of his hand.

Ben had been with the company longer than Remy. In fact, Ben was going on thirty years at the place. A rugged, tall man in his early sixties he was still relatively young looking, the only thing betraying his age was his naturally graying hair. A loyal employee, he asked for and was granted a position in security after the accident that occurred on the loading dock which left him with a permanent limp. Ben had never questioned the accident or the lack of safety railings that weren't there on the dock during his accident but had been installed after. He just felt that it was part of the job and he was grateful for the opportunity to continue working instead of being forced to go on disability.

Remy continued towards the reception area. Behind the almost four feet high area sat Wendy. "Good morning Mr. Gayo."

"Good morning Wendy" Remy answered.

Wendy was still a child at twenty-one. Being Tom Berne's daughter in accounting gave her a slight familiarity with the company. In fact, that familiarity is what led to her employment at Suncoast. During a company picnic that used to occur every year until the 'incident', the then General Manager, Doug Lipowich spotted Wendy and was determined to recruit her. "She is the right face that I want to present my company!" he declared. From there he tracked down Tom and asked him to convince his daughter to work as the company's receptionist. Of course, it was more a coercing from her father than a convincing. After all, it wasn't every man's daughter that was asked by the General Manager to represent the company. And, who knows, thought Tom, maybe this could lead to advantages for him and his career.

Well, as time continued on, certain things came to light. While Wendy was attractive in her own right, that's where the gifts stopped. Intelligent and adept, unfortunately, she was not. The poor kid couldn't even handle answering the phone. After many attempts to train her to do so, it was decided to hire a phone operator. Rightfully, she should have been let go, however, Doug's ego was such that he refused to concede that he had made an error and instead decided to create a new position of 'Master phone orator' to subvert his ill reason. Now, he still had the personable, attractive, Lolita greeting visitors while the phone was being answered in a professional, thorough manner by another.

Remy made his way to the elevators. He barely glanced around at the lobby surroundings. He had been here so many times it was as if he was sleepwalking. The elevator doors opened and Remy stepped in and punched his floor's button without even looking; ready to start another day of work.

Edward J. Indovina

Chapter 5

The nations shall see your righteousness, and all the kings your glory, and you shall be called by a new name that the mouth of the LORD will give.
Isaiah 62:2

Serafin finally made his way to the front of the line in the Registry room. As he found himself in front of the immigration inspector, the feelings of overpowering intimidation returned. He noticed that the inspector sat behind a large desk on a raised platform. Directly behind the inspector was the American flag and a portrait of George Washington whom Serafin didn't really know. As he approached the inspector he almost felt as though he were at the gates of heaven and answering St. Peter's questions of his earthly indiscretions.

"Name?" barked the inspector. From his height and position the inspector sounded larger than he was. The truth was though, that he was actually a slight built man who, himself, was a child of Irish immigrants. He was, in fact, a true first generation American of the new immigrants who just happened now to be sitting in judgment upon the new immigrant hopefuls.

"Serafin Gayo-Arias, sir." Serafin craned his neck upwards towards the inspector.

"Gayo?" the inspector repeated without looking up from the papers in front of him.

"Yes, Gayo-Arias"

"Ok, Gayo. Do you have any relatives in the United States?"

"No, No sir"

The inspector paused. "So, you speak English?" he asked with his slight Irish accent that was learned from his parents even though he wasn't born in Ireland.

"Yes, I try."

"Well, that is better than most. It makes my job easier" The inspector smiled briefly which broke the illusion of the inspector's eminent superiority to Serafin and actually made him seem human to Serafin and not an intimidating beast.

"Thank you" replied Serafin.

"Did you bring any money? Do you have any medical problems?"

"Yes, I have thirty American dollars and No, I do not have any medical problems, sir"

"What is your political affiliation?"

Serafin was taken aback by this question and hesitated before he answered.

"Pardon, I mean... what?"

"Your politics. Are you an anarchist, socialist, communist?"

"Ummm... I really have no affiliation. If you mean do I believe in the politics of my old country, that is no. There is a reason I am leaving it behind..."

The inspector looked at Serafin and smiled.

"So, what you are telling me is that you believe in Democracy, right?" The inspector was clearly steering Serafin to an answer that he could note favorably.

"Ummm... Si, Yes, yes."

"Congratulations Serafin Gayo, you are granted passage into the United States. Good Luck" The inspector stamped Serafin's paperwork with authority.

Serafin looked upwards to the inspector. "Gracias, Thank you."

Serafin was so relieved that he forgot to notice that he had lost the name of Arias to his surname. He took his card and moved forward.

Serafin thought about what had just happened. It was obvious that the inspector had displayed kindness towards him, but he wondered about the politics question. The one thing that he didn't realize about his new country was about the circling political and public winds about immigrants in the United States at the time.

America was experiencing a strong wave of antiradical hysteria among its 'native' inhabitants. As time went on this wave became known as the Red Scare. With the widespread labor unrest and the emergence of Communism in Russia, Hungary and the Eastern European Theater, the citizens of the United States were starting to get worried that it was only a matter of time before those scary oppressive movements hit their shores.

Meanwhile, the Attorney General of the United States, A. Mitchell Palmer, was directing the arrest of thousands of suspected radicals in the country. Those that were aliens were directed to be deported immediately. However, regardless of Palmer's efforts to quell the public's fears of immigrants and their politics, the series of bombings that occurred in 1919 by a group known as 'The American Anarchists' simply gave credence and reality to the 'Red Scare'.

It became worse in April of 1919 when another bomb plot was uncovered. This plot consisted of sending a series of dynamite bombs to individuals on the anarchists' enemy list. One of those on the list was the Attorney General, Palmer himself. Scores of people who were involved either by association or suspicion with the anarchists were arrested or detained with no due process in an effort to quell the plot. Yet, as these people were rounded up it began to become known that many of them were of Mexican and Italian origin which only served to scare the American people even further.

The most infamous of these anarchists were Ferdinando Sacco and Bartolomeo Vanzetti. They were Italian immigrants and self-proclaimed anarchists who belonged to a group known as the Galleanist Anarchists. Unfortunately for these two, they were implicated on suspicion and association of a prior robbery and murder due to their association with the group. The two of them became the poster children for the Red Scare and, despite circumstantial evidence at best, they were tried in the public forum, and due to the public outcry and hysteria about the anarchists, were eventually sentenced to death for their crimes in a federal court. Clearly it was not an opportune time to be a European immigrant in America.

Serafin, having heard some of it over in his native Spain, did not let it deter him and he happily went to the train boarding station.

Serafin got off on the train heading towards the city of Rochester. It wasn't easy for him because he felt as though he was being dishonest. He had noted on the ship's manifest that he was staying with a friend, Antonio Lorenzo, in Brooklyn, NY. Thus, he slipped onto the train headed for Rochester with the porters not paying attention, or at least he thought. As he paid his fare he sat in the center of the car with his hat down. Of course, Serafin didn't realize that it really meant nothing to the train porters where he went.

In fact, it meant nothing to anyone he would encounter. In this country, the peering eyes were gone, unlike what had begun to occur in his native land. Here, it was every man for themselves. If you made it, or if you failed, everything was all upon yourself.

The train ride actually served to be therapeutic to Serafin. Its long and monotonous ride actually would serve to help him to relax slightly. While he still felt the trepidation and guilt for leaving his home, the repetitive thuds of the wheels on the tracks placed him in an almost trans-meditative state which served to ease his mind and body. The ship ride had been almost too tumultuous which he didn't begin to fully realize until he had finally begun to relax.

Serafin drifted off into sleep. As he began to swell into the welcoming stage of REM the dreams started.

Serafin found himself gazing from a vantage above a funeral procession. The view was as if it were a modern camera angle from atop the roof tops. Straining to focus he couldn't quite make out the people on the street in the procession. Then, he saw it. Squinting his eyes (even though he wasn't, it was a dream) he made out his brother, Maggiore, and his brother Pedro leading the procession. They were dressed in ceremonial robes and were spraying the gathered crowd with holy water as they progressed. The coffin immediately behind them was of black lacquer and gold hardware.

As Serafin concentrated on the procession it came to a stop within the cemetery. The coffin bearers brought the casket to the poles above the previously dug burial hole and rested it atop. As his brothers performed the ritualistic rites they stood before the tombstone and obscured its view from Serafin. After the last prayer was recited the brothers stepped aside and revealed the stone. Serafin viewed the stone anxiously. On the left side was carved in the stone, 'Amado Esposo, Ramiel' Serafin started to shake in his sleep.
This couldn't be. This was the funeral for his mother. And he was nowhere to be seen, he couldn't even attend her funeral! He had abandoned her!

Serafin woke with a start. Sweat was pouring down his head and across his whole body. "NO!" he screamed as he woke. The other passengers quickly turned their attention to him and then looked away. In the meantime, a coachman and another passenger made their way to him.

"Excuse me sir. Is everything ok?" the coachman asked politely.

"Si, si... Estoy bien" Serafin answered in his native tongue.

"Um... is that good?" the coachman asked. While he had many foreign passengers he never attempted to try to understand their languages.

Serafin recovered. "Yes, I am fine, thank you. I apologize for disturbing you."

The coachman nodded politely. "It is fine, sir. Try to enjoy the rest of your trip."

As the coachman walked away Serafin took a deep breath. As he began to compose himself, the other passenger approached.

She was an older woman of perhaps fifty or so. Heavy in stature, she radiated a calm, nurturing aura. She bent her head down to the still seated Serafin and tilted his fedora up and smiled into his eyes. He felt a wave of relief over him as the matronly fresh face framed in black hair spoke to him.

"Pardon. I... couldn't help but overhear. estas bien?"

Serafin began to focus. "Si, si. Muchas gracias... eh.."

"Carmen, Carmen Ustevedes."

"I am happy to meet you Carmen. I am sorry to disturb you."

"Eh... no es nada." She smiled. "Actually, it broke the monotony of this ride"

Serafin embarrassedly smiled. "Si, supongo que si."

Carmen smiled again and placed her hand on his shoulder.

"It will be alright, estar a gusto. I sense a good heart in you. Remember, el senor se ocupa de su propia."

Serafin relaxed, "Gracias, gracias. You are right."

Carmen stood and started towards her seat.

"Relax young one. I am here if you need me"

With that Carmen sat in her seat with a final look towards Serafin.

The train came to a stop. "All departing for Rochester, NY!" the conductor yelled out.

Serafin stood up, adjusted his coat and grabbed his suitcase. Here it was. The place he had chosen to start a new life in his new adopted country.

As he disembarked from the train he began to realize that he needed to find a place to stay. The adventure of arriving was coming to a close and the reality of setting up a place to live was beginning. As he entered the train station lobby and looking around he noticed that the Train station was actually a half-way point for many travelers. Many of them used the train station as their sleeping quarters until they either found a place or move to the shelters that were set up for them.

He began to read the bulletin boards at the train station for a room flier. He had started to teach himself English a year before he left in anticipation of his journey. His English wasn't bad but he was much better at his native Spanish or even Italian which he learned as a second language to help his mother with the travelers that often came to their hometown. Like most of his countrymen, being adept and learning more than one language was of importance to him.

Many people traveled between countries in Europe and it made things easier to be fluent in more than one language. As he scanned the board his eyes fell upon a note written in Italian. A room was available at a house on Central Avenue. Serafin grabbed the note and went inside to inquire on directions to get to the home.

Chapter 6

Remy got off of the elevator on the fourth floor. The fourth floor was the sales department and customer support floor. Remy had been on this floor for close to six years now. He turned right down the hallway, stopped at the refreshment center; and poured himself a cup of coffee then proceeded to his office.

As he entered his office, once again he barely looked around. He had been in here so many times he felt as though he could navigate through it as though he were blind. To the right of the door was his coat rack, a gift from Rachiel when he first got the transfer to the Sales department. Towards the left was a book rack which contained many of the product and specifications manuals that he used to use. Actually, many of those manuals were outdated and the more current manuals were accessible from his PC. However, he kept the books because of their appearance.

"It looks professional" Remy thought to himself. Towards the center of the room and approximately seventy percent into the room was his desk. It was a modern desk with a glass top and no drawers.

'No clutter makes for efficient employees' was the efficiency consultant's motto as he re-designed all the furniture in the building. The joke was that while no one kept clutter on their desk it was kept on all of the surrounding areas. It was a similar theory to the 'Paperless Office' which had the paradoxical effect of creating more paper as people printed more than one copy from their electronic storage devices because they could.

Remy hung up his windbreaker on the coat rack, proceeded to his desk with his cup of coffee in hand, and grabbed the mouse computer. The first thing he did was check his e-mail in the morning.

It was becoming more common that the vast majority of Remy's clients communicated by e-mail nowadays, instead of by phone. Remy didn't mind, in fact, he actually embraced it. Granted, it made things slightly more impersonal, but it was definitely more efficient and accurate. Instead of playing 'phone tag' one could make sure that their message was sent. And, this meant from wherever they were. No longer were people tied to a desk or an office.

Heck, Remy knew that many of his clients conducted 'business' while on the golf course or on a fishing boat. Although those were luxuries he wasn't able to take part in.

The one thing that Remy did notice in this world of increasing anonymity is how people's manners seemed to start turning downward. He observed that when a client was upset or disappointed the language they used was harsher in an electronic communiqué than it was when on a telephone. Did this expansion of communication in society yield nasty habits due to the faceless make-up of the message? How far would this demeanor go? Remy remembered his father lamenting about the age of nuclear weapons and how easy it was to push a button to kill hundreds of thousands of faceless people. Now, people were able to vehemently and cruelly berate someone anonymously and with no repercussions. This almost seemed to be the next logical extension of that behavior.

Remy scanned his e-mail. "Cool" he thought, he had just taken an order for 40,000 protective covers from a client in India. "Yep, this is great. I remember when I didn't have a chance in hell to sell overseas. Now, I can do it every day!" Remy printed the order and continued scanning.

He noticed and opened an e-mail from corporate headquarters.

"Hmm, I wonder what this is?" Perhaps it was another sexual harassment awareness meeting or a note to remember to vote for their 'preferred' political candidate, Remy thought sarcastically.

The e-mail read, "Meeting in boardroom A at 2:00 pm for all associates. Attendance is mandatory!" The note almost screamed out at him.

"Well, I guess I can't take a late lunch" Remy mused to himself. The anticipated trepidation from the corporate e-mail soon faded. He thought about the recent order he had taken from overseas. The order for 40,000 covers was great news. Sales had been off this year and the order would help his department to recover slightly from their fallen projections. The international economy hadn't been strong and to obtain an order like this was encouraging news, at least that's what Remy thought. He finished perusing the e-mails and got up. Remy headed over to his boss's office to tell him the good news.

Chapter 7

Serafin stepped out of the Taxi, paid the driver and approached the home on the flier. He stood at the edge of the street and looked down the paved walk towards the house. He nervously took a step on the walk and proceeded towards the house. As he arrived at the front door of the house he paused a second before knocking on the door. He anxiously double checked the address of the home to the notice he had taken off of the bulletin board at the train station. It was the same. He adjusted his overcoat and made sure that his hat was sitting straight. He rapped on the door three times in succession.

As Serafin waited for a response to his call he stepped back a step and took a look at the home. It was a two-story home and very similar to the other houses that lined the street. An American Colonial style, it featured asphalt shingles and an upper window in the attic area. The shingles were painted a pale green and the trim and windows were painted white. On the left was a single driveway and towards the rear was a garage. At the side of the house towards the driveway was a side entrance door and a small milk delivery door.

As the heavy wooden door swung open a stout looking middle aged man appeared. About five-foot-six-inches tall he appeared to be about 160 pounds. Burly and strong looking he examined Serafin from head to toe with his kind, yet piercing brown eyes which were framed by his bulbous nose and slightly graying black hair.

"Buongiorno, signore" Serafin answered. He tilted his hat in recognition of his potential host.

The owner of the house continued to look Serafin up and down questioningly. He noticed that this young man, slightly taller than himself, was dressed well, despite the wrinkled and traveled appearance of the clothes.

"Cosa posso fare per voi?"

"Eh, Vedo che avete una stanza in affitto"

The homeowner gave Serafin one last look and replied "Si. you want to see it?"

The sudden change to English struck Serafin by surprise. But, he recovered quickly. "Yes, Yes I would please."

"Molto Buono." the owner smiled ear to ear. He knew that he tried to trip up Serafin and he failed to do so. Serafin passed the test which the homeowner had a gut feeling he would. He invited Serafin inside. "Come. I show you the room."

Serafin followed the man into the home. Serafin removed his hat and walked inside.

As Serafin entered the home he noticed the others in the room. Behind the man to the right was an older woman about the age of the home owner. Seated on the chair and couch directly behind them were two young girls. One was approximately 14 and the other was about 16. They were very pretty and attracted Serafin's eye, especially the younger one. The room was a sitting room. Towards the center of the room was a couch and to its left was a recliner chair. Next to the recliner was a small table with an ashtray.

Towards the rear of the room was a large console radio. Serafin had heard of radios but had never seen one. His mind raced at the wonders and riches of this country. The owner of the house noticed Serafin's mind wandering and broke the silence.

"Il mio nome è Bruno Santangelo. E tu sei?"

Serafin broke out of his trance induced by the daughter and room and blurted out "Estoy Serafin" as he spoke he realized that he used his native language.

Bruno placed his hands on his chin and spoke. "Hmmm.. so, you are a Spaniard?"

"Umm.. Si." Serafin recovered quickly and answered him in Italian. "Fa che ha sconvolto voi?"

A hearty laugh came out of Bruno and his whole body seemed to shake, " No! No it does not. In fact, I have to say, I am, umm... impressionato, impressed. You think well on your feet. You are quite well versed!"

Serafin was nervous and self-conscious suddenly. All eyes were on him. He didn't know if this was false praise or genuine.

Bruno sensed this and sought to put the young man at ease. "Serafin, this is my humble family. Mia moglie, Regina. Mia figlia Verotta and Petrina."

The girls smiled and waved from the couch that they were seated backwards on with their elbows on the backrest as their names were called.

Bruno's wife, Regina, was a strong looking woman. Robust and hale looking she was approximately five-feet-four inches, one-hundred-forty pounds with dark features. Her dark hair and round face revealed her ethnic origins from Messina, in Sicily.

Bruno and Regina's daughters were attractive girls in their own right. Verotta favored her mother while Petrina, her father. Both girls had dark features similar to their parents and were of average height. Verotta was the same height as her mother while Petrina was also at the same height. Petrina, being younger, was obviously going to pass up her sister and mother in stature. The girls' facial features were very attractive with the strong cheekbones and narrow noses that came from their ethnic origins.

Bruno and Regina had emigrated to the United States nine years prior. Originally from Messina, Sicily, the family left Italy as the political climate darkened in the country. It wasn't the first time that Bruno had moved. Originally from Erice, he moved to Messina when he was sixteen. It was there that he met Regina and started their family.

When Bruno first laid eyes on Regina he was fascinated. Her features appeared to him as exotic and captivating. As a native of Messina, Regina enjoyed the highlights of the many races that had inhabited that area over the ages. Located on the Northeastern side of Sicily, Messina was actually founded by the Greeks and subsequently conquered by numerous others in part due to Its advantageous position on the straight. While Bruno felt that he had found the life he wished, the earthquake that hit Messina in 1908 was as though a sign from God to finally leave his homeland.

Bruno turned to his guest. "Serafin, you seem like a nice young man. Do not worry, as long as you take my advice. In this country we are all the same. Not one of the people who live in this country are native, despite what they tell you. This is a beautiful land of immigrants and far be it from me to judge a fellow immigrant despite what area of Europe they came from. We are all equal here, however, as long as you work hard and give back to the ones who help. Remember, the Lord helps those who help themselves and others!"

Serafin relaxed a bit and noticed that the younger daughter, Petrina, smiled approvingly. He turned his attention to Bruno.

"So, will you show me the room?"

"That depends. Do you have a job?"

"No, not yet. But I will"

Bruno smiled, "Va bene. I came over myself with dreams and hopes. Come, the rent is four dollars a month, including meals from my lovely wife. Regina looked at Serafin and nodded approvingly.

"Tomorrow you will accompany me to my place of work and ask for employment."

Bruno motioned Serafin up the stairs to show him the room under the watchful eyes of Bruno's daughters.

Chapter 8

Remy walked down the hall towards his supervisor's office. As Remy entered his boss's office he approached Shelly, his boss's secretary. Shelly was an attractive woman, approximately Rachiel's age. Her green eyes and dyed blonde hair belied her true features, though. While Remy didn't know for sure, he guessed that Shelly's true hair color was brown, like her eyebrows. Yet, he thought, he had seen many a blonde haired woman with black eyebrows that came from the northern area of Italy, like his aunt Carmine, so, who was he to say.

Shelly was seated at her desk directly in front of the boss's office. The outer office was modestly decorated with four stand-up plants, a seating couch and, what appeared to be obligatory in most offices now-a-days, framed pictures with 'inspirational' sayings. Posters that display a scenic photograph with a business buzz word beneath it, 'Attitude: A positive attitude is a powerful force-it can't be stopped!' Remy always smirked when he saw them.

Remy stopped by the front of Shelly's desk.

"Hey, Shel, how's John?" John was Shelly's husband. Remy and John got to know each other on some mutual fishing trips. In fact, it was Shelly that had introduced them at an office party and the two of them had hit it off. They had a lot of mutual interests and became good friends.

"He's good, Remy. In fact, have you talked to him lately? He thinks he's in line for a promotion at the Bank!"
Remy smiled broadly at her.

"Really? That's great! He's a good guy, I hope he gets it! Then he can buy the beers for the boat!"

Shelly smirked. "Yeah, he said you would say that"

"Is the boss in? I want to run something by him"

"Yeah" Shelly turned her voice low, "but he's real quiet. Something's on his mind."

Remy smiled openly.

"Well, maybe I can bring him out of it. I've got good news."

Shelly looked back down at her paperwork.

"I Hope so, go on in," she motioned with her head without looking.

Remy rapped on the door before he entered. Remy had always envied Bill's office, not Bill, just his office. Remy and Bill had started at about the same time with the company.

In fact, both of them worked for a brief time on the loading docks. However, unlike Remy, Bill had a Bachelor's degree from Roberts Wesleyan College and was merely on the docks as an entry position. Remy always felt that Bill was given the privileged track in reflection to Remy's work track. Yet, deep down Remy understood that Bill had worked hard towards his degree and was perhaps entitled to a jump start. Still, trying to understand that didn't remove his feelings of envy. As a Sales Manager, Bill commanded twice the area of the company base salesmen's offices. In addition to the obligatory bookshelves and racks, Bill's office contained its own wet bar. Actually it was called a refreshment bar but if you looked in the bottom shelves there was the requisite alcohol as it was in the 1960's. As he entered, Bill was staring intently at his large flat screen computer monitor screen.

Remy broke the silence. "Um.. Hey Bill. Sorry to bother you but..."

Bill Adams looked up as if he woke from a trance. He was dressed, as usual, in an impeccably tailored suit, yet, even though it was first thing in the morning, it had a curiously rumpled look. Bill looked at Remy before responding and Remy noticed his tired looking eyes. "Oh, Remy. How are you? What can I do for you?"

Remy also noted the formality in Bill's voice. Now, he was nervous himself. Remy took a breath, swelled his chest slightly as he prepared himself to deliver his announcement.

"Well, I just wanted to tell you that the firm in India placed an order for 40,000 covers. Isn't that great?" The words spilled out as though he was auditioning for an auctioneer spot.

Bill averted his glance "Yeah, yeah. Good work Remy." he paused and continued as though he hadn't heard Remy's announcement. " Ummm.. did you get the notice about the meeting?"

Remy stared at Bill and tilted his head. "Umm...Yeah, I did"

Without looking up Bill replied indifferently. "Good, I just want to make sure you're there"

"Will do, Bill" Remy could sense the aversion and excused himself out. He exited Bill's office and proceeded into the outer office occupied by Shelly. As he walked by Shelly's desk he leaned in towards her, nodded and whispered, "I see what you mean. See you later" Shelly nodded as she continued doing her work pretending not to hear Remy.

Remy made his way to his office to prepare the order sheets for shipping of the order.

Chapter 9

Serafin looked around the room. It was compact but had enough area to contain in addition to a bed and a dresser, a seating chair and nightstand. Bruno's wife had decorated the room smartly.

As he entered, the stand-up dresser was to the right, the bed in the center of the room while the nightstand and seating chair towards the left side. There was enough room to maneuver in the room and an added extra was the small closet next to the dresser. Serafin hung up his jacket, shirt, and trousers in the closet and lay down on the bed.

Serafin had a huge grin on his face as he lay down and attempted to close his eyes to sleep.

Of course, he couldn't sleep and spent most of the night folding his clothes and placing them in order in the drawers. Every time he lay down on the small bed his mind raced terribly. He was nervous and excited at the same time, once again. One part of him started counting down the balance of money that he had remaining and the other part started to get excited about the possibility of working and making money in this country.

Before he knew it the sun's rays peered through the window. As he rose, he kneeled beside his bed and said a silent prayer. His meditation was broken by a sudden loud voice.

"Buongiorno!" the cry came from the bottom of the stairs.

Serafin had already gotten out of bed. He had gotten dressed earlier and had just lay down waiting for the morning. As he reached for the door a sharp rap sounded on his door accompanied by a girl's voice.

"Affrettatevi! Padre doesn't like to wait!"

As Serafin opened the door he saw the back of Petrina's head race down the stairs. Serafin followed her down the stairs and entered the kitchen area.

"Ah, buongiorno Serafin." Bruno spoke. "Sedersi." Bruno motioned with his hand as he was seated in his chair.

Serafin looked around and nodded at everyone. He waited until the girls were seated before he took his seat. He pulled his chair towards the edge of the table and arranged his napkin on his lap. His hands were tucked in towards his side and he waited patiently.

Bruno smiled and nodded his head animatedly. He leaned forward in his chair.

"Bene, Nice. You have good manners. La tua familigia ha fatto un buon lavoro!"

Serafin nodded his head as he blushed slightly. "Grazie."

Then, from in front of the stove arose a voice that sounded like thunder. It was as though a Valchiria had come down from the heavens.

"Enough, Bruno! Leave the boy alone!" She turned her attention towards Serafin. "Now, never mind that Asinello. Mangia, you have a big day ahead of you!" She emphasized her words by waving a spoon in the air like a sword.

The girls looked at each other and down while suppressing a giggle. Bruno may have thought he was the king of the household but everyone knew really that it was Regina that made everyone hop to attention.

Bruno ducked his head in mock obedience.

"Mi scusi. I did not realize that this boy was under your protection mi Regina!" Bruno laughed loud and clear after saying this.

Regina glared at Bruno playfully. She dished the eggs out of the cast iron pan and served her family to their plates. As she plated Bruno's servings she offered him a scowl of remandance.

While they ate, Bruno once again addressed Serafin. "Now, present yourself well. When I introduce you to the foreman he will be studying you like a hawk examines his prey. Remember, you work hard, you succeed in this country. Not like where you came from! There is no one here to hold you back, regardless of what you feel. But, also remember, you reap what you sow in this country. If you choose to work in a mediocre manner then you will achieve mediocre things. And, if you expect to raise a family in this country, half way is no way here."

Serafin nodded intently. He trusted Bruno, he did not know why or how, but he knew that he did.

Bruno finished his breakfast and stood up before Serafin had finished his. "Now, we are done. Come! Take your coat and hat and come with me to the Railroad."

Serafin hurriedly rose and placed his napkin on his plate. "Grac..Grazie, Regina."

A smile came across Regina's face. "La vostra accoglienza, Serafin. Ora, andate. Fare una buona impressione! Make your mother proud!"

Bruno had begun placing his coat upon himself in the foyer while his family gathered around him.

Serafin watched as Bruno kissed both of his daughters and his wife goodbye. "Hmm, maybe this is how it is supposed to be." he thought. As they proceeded out the door Serafin caught the eyes of

Petrina watching him and waving as he left the house.

Edward J. Indovina

Chapter 10

"Thy tongue deviseth mischiefs; like a sharp razor, working deceitfully. Thou lovest evil more than good; and lying rather than to speak righteousness. Selah. Thou lovest all devouring words, O thou deceitful tongue."
Psalms 52:2-4

The employees of Suncoast East filled the meeting room. The meeting room was as everything in this building, typical of most modern office buildings meeting rooms. Twelve tables filled the room with approximately six chairs per table. The chairs were on one side with everything designed to face forward towards the front of the room. At the front of the room was a fold out white dry erase board which also served to perform as a projector screen. Recessed into the ceiling was a large plasma screen that was utilized for inter-office communications between branches. The screen was in the down position with a company logo broadcast upon it.

It was a standing room only situation as everyone squeezed in to the room. Mumbling and speculation filled the room. The company, Suncoast, as it grew, embraced the new technologies of video conferencing. This allowed the company to address its two main offices without flying executives across the country. It also enabled them to convey the company messages on a simultaneous platform. Now, there was no danger in creating rumors if a meeting was held at headquarters in Wyoming and then two days later in Rochester. Real time messaging was an advantage in this age.
Remy squeezed into the room at the rear and positioned himself between his co-workers.

"Hey, what do you think? Did we buy the other plant?" John in purchasing questioned Remy.

Remy was towards the back of the room leaning on the wall. He looked over the room and observed his fellow employees. Some had a look of scared anticipation while others appeared indifferent and bothered by the intrusion to their normal day. It was safe to conclude that no one was devoid of an opinion towards this meeting.

Remy responded to John's question.

"I don't know. But I don't think so. It's been slow lately, but I took a good sized order today."

"Hey, that's great! But do you think..." John trailed off as the video screen went live.

The room reduced to a hush as the vision of the company's CEO appeared on the screen.

He was seated at a desk dressed in tailored gray suit with a white shirt and blue print tie. Behind him was a generic office background replete with bookshelves on either side of him while directly behind him was the Suncoast logo with an American flag to the left of it. He motioned to the monitor with his head and began speaking.

"Ladies and Gentlemen, Welcome, and thank you for taking time from your designated duties today."

John Giles, the CEO, came to Suncoast from General Electric just last year. When he arrived it was with much fanfare and anticipation. During his stint with G.E. he was known for his cost cutting adeptness and his production skills. He served as Vice President of development in the medical technologies section of G.E. While he had advanced press of a positive sort, the rumblings began to surface of his political lobbying skills and the indifference he felt towards the employees. Despite his tenure of almost a year, thus far he had really made no discernible impact on Suncoast, slight of the Federal grant of $560 million he procured to support the switch from optical lenses to Solar panel technology. In reality, the employees knew too little of the man and saw too little in improvements to form a positive opinion of the man. Granted, the transition from optics to solar was still too early to judge but the employees felt nothing. The rumors were started that with Giles' association with G.E. that he was merely positioning the company to be bought out by G.E. and that would result in a big payout to him and fear and uncertainty to everyone else in the company.

Giles appeared on screen impeccably dressed and coiffed. While the employees didn't feel as though he had done anything to improve their company he certainly looked the part. He took a visible breath and addressed the audience.

"I am well aware of that most of you are curious to the purpose of this meeting, but rest assured that will become clear shortly. Now, let me begin by thanking all of you for your efforts and cooperation for the past few months. Changing company direction is never an easy task. But, you, the people, have made this easier than most."

A collective sigh of relief arose from the room. Remy had a feeling of sickening cynicism wash over him with Giles' introduction.

"Yet, with the ease of transition also comes the pitfalls that often accompany such change."

The room stood still. In fact, all of the side conversations ceased also, as if Giles himself was in the room. Giles continued his oration.

"As most of you are aware, we applied for, and were accepted for, a federal grant for our change in business strategy. Now, again, I'm sure most of you who have been with the company for a while realize that as an optical firm we were struggling. Defense contracts were coming to a close and the reduction in military deployments meant a reduction in the need for our product. Thus, attempting to remain competitive in a rapidly increasing global marketplace began to take its toll on our business. After conversing with consultant and government officials we determined that converting to a solar technology firm appeared to be the proper strategy to take. It wouldn't take much to re-tool our plants to produce solar energy equipment and it would give us a foothold in a viable, growing market."

The hush of the room changed into a growing murmur. The crowd didn't feel right about the words being said. Something was up and everyone sensed it.

"Now, be assured, that the decision to adapt into a solar energy company was not whimsical. In fact, we conferred with top government experts to ensure that we were doing the right thing for us as a company and you, as our valued employees."

The room paused again. The second Remy heard the reference towards government he shook his head in disgust. Now, the murmuring started aloud and in earnest.

Remy was nonplussed by Giles' speech. "Oh, boy, here it comes" he muttered as he watched the monitor.

"Now, be assured, the government wouldn't just give out money to losing causes. Green energy is the growth industry of the future. Studies and experts have shown us such. In fact, experts say that every day that we hesitate in changing we will defer the opportunity to achieve change. The longer we wait the more likely we would become a company that would go the way of the dinosaurs. By following the recommendations of the government experts we would be ensured of survival for our company and employees. Eventually, removing ourselves from dependency on foreign oil will be a necessity for our country as a whole."

Giles paused and stared at the screen. The employees watching the broadcast in Rochester felt as if he were in the room with him presently. Many held their breath in anticipation of his next statement. Melissa towards the rear of the room started to sob. Remy started muttering to himself. "Stupid bastards, they were sold a bill of goods by this ignorant, self-serving, waste of a Federal government!"

Giles straightened his tie on camera and continued; however, this time he didn't look the camera with his eyes. It was suddenly as if Giles could see the Rochester audience listening to his speech and experience what they were feeling. The balance of his talk was conducted looking either down at his prop desk or towards the side.

"Unfortunately, as sometimes happens with great plans, we seem to have slightly miscalculated and our present business model does not appear to be no longer feasible. As much as we reconsidered various options, many of them did not prove viable. Eventually we reached a conclusion aided by Federal economic experts. Current economic conditions, which our government leaders inherited from their predecessors, have made our planned business model unsuitable at the present time. In addition, the worldwide recession and slow down of markets abroad have also been a burden upon our corporation. Thus, I am sad to announce, that we will be forced to shut our doors, effective this coming Friday."

As he said this he looked down dejectedly at the top of his desk. A pin could be heard to drop in the room.

Giles took a visible deep breath and continued.

Remy muttered in the meantime, "and the Academy Award for Lying Bastard goes to..."

Giles wrapped up his broadcast. "Now, I'm sure many of you have numerous questions regarding your future and your severance. Rest assured that we at Suncoast appreciate and understand your situations. Your supervisors will be able to answer most of your questions but I will lay out the main points of your severance."

By now there were disgruntled groans, growing anger, and despair amongst the attendees. Many of the audience had stopped listening and loud conversations were being conducted among the meeting audience. Audible sobbing and lamenting was also heard amongst the attendees.

"While we realize that this is terribly disruptive to most of you, we ask that you appreciate the measures we have extended towards you, our valued associates, throughout these unfortunate circumstances. You may rest assured that our decisions were influenced by our consummate recognition of the contributions towards our achievement as a major company worldwide."

"You disingenuous son-of-a-bitch" Remy thought to himself.

The viewing audience was stunned. Even the sobbing employees ceased and stared at the screen.

Giles adjusted his hair and tie and visibly breathed while he continued. "The aforementioned being said, we ask your cooperation as follows:"

"OoooKay..." John muttered purposely aloud.

"One, we ask that everyone stay on for the next two weeks to help us close the plant. It would not look good upon us if we were just to appear to abandon the facility. Two, you will all be eligible for unemployment benefits. As most of you are aware, the government has extended unemployment benefits for up to 99 weeks. This should help most of you during the transition."

"Niiice... How convenient that the company shuts its doors just as the government extends unemployment benefits. Now the bastards will be off the hook for that expense when they file for bankruptcy," Remy thought bitterly.

"Finally, many of you will be eligible for a government grant of $13,000 for those of you who wish to retrain into another field."

Remy was beside himself. While the others in the room were discussing their relief or their sorrow, Remy noted to himself that he was damn sure that Giles and the rest of his cronies were going to walk away with a nice pillow of cash.

"I would like to repeat, thank you one and all for your dedication and efforts."

With that the screen went to a still picture of the three bullet points that Giles had just recited. The din in the room rose and Remy felt like he had just been hit in the gut.

Chapter 11

Whatever you do, work heartily, as for the Lord and not for men.
Colossians 3:23

The public transportation bus pulled up in front of the railroad. Bruno nudged Serafin in his seat. "Vieni! This is our stop!"

Serafin rose from the padded seat and followed Bruno down the aisle towards the front of the bus. As he walked down the steps he turned towards the drive and thanked him. The driver adjusted his hat and smiled at him.

Serafin followed Bruno off the bus and towards the front doors of the railroad office. He self-consciously grabbed at his hat and adjusted his jacket. Bruno glanced back and laughed.

"Serafin, relax!" Bruno put his hand on his shoulder, "You'll be fine, just remember what I told you!"

Bruno opened the doors to the Railroad office and Serafin followed. As they entered, Serafin took a look around.

The lobby of the Railroad office was huge to the young man from Spain. The shiny tile floors made the room appear to be that much larger than it really was. Directly in front of the doors, set back about thirty feet was the reception desk. Seated at the reception desk was a pretty red-head young lady in a smart looking gray suit. She deftly handled the company switchboard while greeting the incoming employees and visitors.

"Good Morning Mr. Santangelo," the woman announced as Bruno walked towards the desk.

"Buongiorno, Lucy," Bruno replied. Bruno motioned towards his companion, "Lucy, this is my friend, Serafin."

Serafin was taken aback by the use of the word 'friend.' Perhaps he really had made an impression with Bruno.

"Oh, well, good morning to you also, Mr. Serafin" Lucy smiled widely as she answered the telephone while routing another call. She operated the switchboard mechanism like a pro. Each call was routed by inserting the proper phone cable jack into the appropriate receptacle.

"Thank you." Serafin tipped his hat towards Lucy. Meanwhile, Bruno was already heading down the hall and Serafin increased the pace of his gait to catch up to him. Serafin was beginning to find out that when Bruno wanted to move, he moved, regardless of his companions accompanying him.

Bruno and Serafin continued down the hall towards their destination, of which, Serafin was clueless. As they continued down the painted concrete block walls they passed numerous open offices and gathering rooms. The rooms and offices were occupied by different employees of the Railroad.

"Buongiorno Bruno!" numerous men said as they walked by. "eh, Buongiorno!" Bruno replied readily and happily as he led Serafin towards the office of the supervisor.

Bruno knocked on the open door of his supervisor's office and announced himself. The door was a heavy wooden door with a smoked glass window that took up the upper half of the door. In painted script were the words: "Supervisor, Giuseppe Santini'.

"Scusi, Giuseppe, do you have a minute?" Bruno asked as he entered the office.

Giuseppe had his back to the men as they entered the room. Serafin couldn't quite make it out but it appeared that Giuseppe was preparing a beverage of some sort at the credenza located directly behind his desk. As Serafin approached he noticed the espresso pot on a silver tray located on top of the credenza.

Without turning around Giuseppe answered Bruno. "Naturalmente, un minuto."

Serafin noticed that from the rear Giuseppe appeared to be about in his mid thirties. His dark hair and slender build betrayed his true age. Although he attempted to carry himself as more mature, it was not the case. Giuseppe wore a well tailored and fine fabric suit. His taste in clothing said a lot about him, His shoes were well polished and of Italian origin. While he was hunched over his cup of espresso he appeared to stand about five feet six inches in height.

Giuseppe Santini finally straightened up and turned around; he looked Serafin up and down as Bruno had said he would.

Bruno broke the silence, "Giuseppe, this is my friend Serafin. He just recently arrived here and is staying with me." Bruno paused. "Eh, and I was thinking that he could work on the docks in the pits."

"You mean the coal duty, don't you?" Giuseppe corrected Bruno.

While many of the workers called the coal storage bins the 'pits', he didn't like to denigrate the job. After all, if it wasn't for the workers who managed the coal the cities would have no power. And, besides, on the docks were where Giuseppe himself started.

Giuseppe was still examining Serafin as he replied to Bruno. He noticed that while Serafin's clothing was worn, it was clean and well pressed. He also noticed that Serafin's shirt was very white and clean, his slacks pressed well, and his shoes, while well traveled, were freshly polished. Giuseppe respected the fact that Serafin took pride in his appearance, as he did.

"Ciao." Serafin extended his hand to Giuseppe's, "E 'un piacere conoscerti Giuseppe."

Giuseppe hardened his stare at Serafin and shook his extended hand. "Well, you speak Italiano, eh?"

Serafin nodded eagerly. "Si, I speak English also"

Giuseppe grasped his chin with his left hand and cocked his head towards Serafin. "Hmmm, where are you from Serafin?"

"Sant Tome, Espana"

Giuseppe's eyes widened with pleasant surprise. "Spagna? You are a Spaniard?"

Serafin nervously swallowed. While Bruno asked the same question of him he felt nervous in front of Giuseppe regarding the fact of his heritage. He smiled weakly and looked Giuseppe in the eye before he answered. He took a deep breath, steeled himself, and stated audaciously. "Si, is that a problem?"

Giuseppe broke from his harsh persona and laughed out loud. His attempt at intimidation worked to a point and then failed when it came to this. "No, no! You are full of fire, aren't you? Bruno, you didn't tell me he was cornuto!"

Bruno smiled and Serafin looked at both of them and grinned also.

Bruno replied between chuckles. "I didn't know myself. Full of fire, full of hard work, eh?"

Giuseppe grinned and nodded in earnest. "Si, I think so. So, Cornuto Serafin, you have no problems working hard, do you?"

"No, signore. I work hard for you if you give me the chance."

Giuseppe smiled but, turned serious; he placed his hand on Serafin's shoulder.

"Serafin, let me tell you. I like you; I get a good feeling about you. You have a fire within you that I admire. But, allow me to tell you something. I came to this country eight years ago with barely anything in my pocket. Perhaps similar to you. I was alone and nervous. Yet, with some help from some fellow immigrants I earned an opportunity at this job and I worked hard. Never a day did I come in to work and not work hard. And, you know what?"

Serafin started to speak but Giuseppe continued.

"I climbed, what they call, the ladder here and eventually worked my way up to be the foreman. With the earnings from my hard work here I also own a home and my wife and children are taken care of. These are things that I could not achieve in my native land. The one thing that I learned is that this country will give you as much as you give it."

Serafin nodded his head in acknowledgement of the message he was given.

Giuseppe removed his hand from Serafin's shoulder and walked towards the front of his desk and leaned himself against it.

"Serafin, again, I do not know why, but I like you. I am going to do for you what was done for me. I will give you a chance. You will start on the docks with the coal hoppers. Now, be forewarned, It is hard work. You will be shoveling coal from the cars into the delivery ships. It is thankless, dirty, work, but, it is work. You want?"

Serafin nodded his head quickly. He could not believe his good fortune. Silently to himself he praised God for his blessing. Finding a place to stay, a job, and help from Bruno and Giuseppe brought a humbling feeling over him. He looked up and repeated his silent prayer and then refocused on Giuseppe.

"Grazie, grazie. I will not let you down. Or Bruno!" he turned to his newfound friend and landlord.

"Good, I also did it as much for Bruno. I wouldn't want him to have to evict you for no money!"

Bruno looked at Giuseppe quizzically. "How.. How did you..."

"Enough, Bruno. Of course I know. But I also know that if you didn't think well of this young man you wouldn't have wasted your time with him!"

Serafin looked at both men and shook their hands eagerly.

Giuseppe once again broke the moment. He addressed both men. "Now, go! I have work to do, and so do you! Bruno, show him how to get to the docks and the locker room. Fretta!"

Serafin and Bruno left the office. Serafin could not believe his good fortune and was determined to repay the kindness shown him.

He wouldn't forget what these good people had given him as an opportunity and vowed to himself to work hard enough to ensure it would last.

Edward J. Indovina

<u>Chapter 12</u>

Remy drove home as if he was in a fog. What was he going to tell Rachiel? For the first time in his marriage, heck, his relationship, he didn't have a job. "What am I going to do? How can I break this to Rach?" he kept repeating to himself.

His mind raced with anxious thoughts. As he was fretting he slammed on the brakes of the car. "Whoa, have to maintain."

Remy realized that he had almost driven into the back of a stopped car. Subconsciously, without even being aware of it, he prevented an accident. His mind was all over the place. "I had better focus or I'm going to really mess up."

He had not even been paying attention to the roads and was essentially driving on auto-pilot until the near accident jolted him aware. He shook his head and proceeded on.

Remy finally noticed his street and eased the car into the driveway. As he pulled into the driveway he noticed that Rachiel's car wasn't there. He hit the steering wheel with the palm of his hand.

"Damn it! I have to go pick up Sari!"

"That wasn't smart, now my freakin' hand hurts," Remy thought to himself angrily. One thing about a steering wheel, he thought. While it may feel cushioned at its core it is a hardened piece of steel and didn't have much give to it. Remy turned his head, looked out the rear window and backed out of the driveway with urgency. He hit the accelerator a little too hard and squealed the tires as he proceeded down the road.

The school was only two miles from their home and he arrived in just a few minutes time. As he passed through the caution light Remy's mind started racing again about the past events of the day. Remy pulled the car up in the drive through in front of the school and waited along with the other parents in their cars.

"Come on, come on. What's taking so long?" Remy started tapping his foot rapidly and his body started shaking involuntarily. Remy realized what he was doing and attempted to calm himself down by squeezing the steering wheel.

"Ok, relax Remy. You're losing it." he thought to himself.

Finally the kids started to come out of the school. Sari walked out of school onto the walk and looked around. Finally, Sari saw the car and ran over to it.

Remy was still preoccupied with himself and didn't notice Sari approaching the car. Sari grabbed for the door handle and quickly yanked open the door, the sudden opening of the door startling Remy.

"Hey dad!" he announced as he plopped himself in the passenger seat. Sari closed the door. Remy had put the car into gear before Sari had fastened his seatbelt and jolted Sari in his seat as he hit the accelerator. Sari adjusted himself and addressed his father,

"Whoa, dad. You ok?"

Remy looked over at his son and smiled weakly and exasperatedly. "Yeah Sari, I'm ok. Just want to get home and eat."

Sari relaxed a bit and responded cheerfully.

"Cool, I can hear that action! I'm starved!"

This time when Remy pulled up to the house, Rachiel's car was there. Rachiel drove a late model American made minivan. While it was only four years old it was starting to reveal its age. The paint on the hood was starting to fade and the inside trim panels were becoming loose. Yet, regardless of the wear on it, it was still reliable. They still owed three years worth of payments on it and they were hoping to replace it before the end of the loan period. However, now with the recent occurrences, Remy thought that it didn't seem likely. Now, the van had better remain reliable. Remy and Sari got out of the car and entered the house.

Remy and Sari took their shoes off in the foyer and before they had a chance to announce themselves Rachiel spoke up.

"Hi honey! Hello, Sari! By the time you're cleaned up I'll have the table set! Hope you don't mind but I picked up pizza for dinner"

"All right!" Sari and Angela said in unison and slapped upraised hands.

Remy stopped and looked at Rachiel. "That's just great. How much did that put us back?"

Rachiel paused and stared at Remy. "Umm, twenty dollars. Why? Is it a problem?"

Remy caught himself and stared blankly past Rachiel. "M'Sorry, just had a rough day. I'll be right there"

Remy went upstairs to the bathroom. As he washed his hands and face, he stared into the mirror. The toll of the day was starting to show on his face. He looked drawn and tired. Remy shook his head and hoped to change his look. He definitely didn't want his family to see him like this. He dried his face off, hung up the tool and went into his bedroom to change his clothes. Remy put on a pair of Jeans and his 'Star Wars' T-shirt.

Remy proceeded down the stairs barefoot and lamely put a smile on his face. As he returned to the kitchen he sat himself at the table and stared at his plate. His plate had two slices of the pizza on it. In the center of the table was the pizza box with the top lid torn off of it. As the kids ate they looked at their father and he, in turn, looked at them quietly. Rachiel broke the silence for all of them and addressed her husband.

"So, anything you want to tell us? Oh, by the way, thanks for picking up Sari."

"The day went fine." Remy looked down as he ate.

Rachiel rolled her eyes and looked at Remy quizzically. Close to twenty years of marriage didn't make her oblivious to her husband's feelings. She knew something was on Remy's mind but she also knew that this wasn't the place to push. She would find out soon enough she determined.

She turned to her children, pizza in hand.

"Okay. Um... kids, how were your days?"

Angela answered first.

"Great mom! I got an 89 on the math quiz and Brittney literally made an ass of herself in gym!"

"Angela! Language!" Rachiel scolded her daughter.

Angela smiled and looked down at the top of table as she continued eating. She answered her mother with a half-full mouth.

"Sorry mom. But, it was just so funny!"

Sari became intrigued at Angela's statement, especially when he heard mention the name of Brittney. Not that he would let on, but Sari had thought Angela's friend Brittney was cute.

"Well, what did she do!?" Sari pressed.

"Oh, of course you want to know. You like her....." Angela replied mockingly.

Sari became suddenly defensive and even appeared to blush slightly.

"Well, why would you say that? I mean, she's ok, and she's your friend. So, why wouldn't I like her? Huh? Why not? What's wrong with that?"

"Yes Angela. What's wrong with that? Now, what did she do?" Rachiel tried to move the conversation along, sensing her husband's demeanor was not typical of him, she was anxious to get to the root of his morose mood.

"Well, today we had to climb the rope, and you know what a bi..., I mean hard it is. So many kids try to pretend that they're sick or hurt just to avoid rope climbing day. Well, anyways, Britt started to climb, got about three scoots up and then bam! She lost her grip and fell right on her butt on the mat. At first we all just looked at her on the mat, and then when we saw she wasn't hurt we all started laughing. Britt got up, looked at us all and then pulled down the back of her shorts and mooned us! I almost died!"

Everyone started laughing at the table but Remy. As their laughter subsided they looked over in the direction of their dad and quieted down.

Remy broke the moment and said: "Well, that wasn't very lady-like was it?"

The laughter started again. Remy broke the mood as he intended. He realized it wasn't right for him to be the downer at the table. Rachiel seemed relieved to hear Remy speak as did the children.

Sari spoke up next.

"Well, I wish I was there, I wouldn't mind seeing Britt's butt!"

"Sari! You're such a pig!" Angela chastised her brother.

"Yes, Serafin Salvatore Gayo. That isn't very nice," Rachiel scolded her son. Whenever Rachiel was angry at her children she used their full names.

Sari defended himself.

"What? I'm just saying!"

"So help me Sari, if you mention a word of this I'll kill you!" Angela screamed.

"Well, does she have a mole or a tattoo?" Sari laughed.

"You'll never know. PIG!" Angela picked up a piece of pizza crust from her plate and flung it at her brother. Even though she was older now she still retained that youthful aversion to crust on her bread.

Remy broke the melee, "All right! Enough already you two! If you're finished go to your rooms and start your homework! Geez, Angela, you did have to bring up your friend's butt to Sari. What did you think would happen?" Remy smirked as the two kids excused themselves and rushed upstairs still bickering.

Rachiel started clearing the table and finally addressed her husband hoping to get him to talk.

"Well, that was interesting. Remember when we were that age?" Rachiel commented as she brought Remy a cup of coffee.

Remy looked down at the table and cradled his cup of coffee with both hands and sighed. "Actually, today, Rach, no, no I don't. I feel old, very old all of a sudden."

Rachiel paused at the sink and sat down at the chair across from her husband at the island. "What's wrong hon?"

"Rach, I don't know how to say it. I've never had this happen to me before."

"What?"

Remy took a deep breath, his eyes welled up with tears and he struggled to get the words out.

"Rach... I, I lost my job."

Rachiel stared in silence. Remy shook nervously in his chair still grasping his coffee and looking down at the counter top.

"I'm sorry Rach, I'm so sorry."

Rachiel broke out of her stupor with a start.

"Why? did you do something wrong?"

Remy caught his breath. "No, hon. No, I didn't. At least I don't think I did." He paused and contemplated suddenly. "I mean, what if it was in part due to me? Maybe if I tried harder sometimes we wouldn't be in this position. What would have happened if I pushed harder to close a deal or follow up with a lead quicker? Maybe the company wouldn't be in this position if I didn't treat my job so lackadaisically at times. Now, now... the company went out of business and shut down and..." He took a deep breath. "I'm out of a job."

Rachiel stared at her husband incredulously and then decisively.

"Well, no matter what you think, that wasn't your fault. You didn't make the big decisions in the boardroom; you didn't change the direction of the company every few years. You did what you were asked, and you did it for the most part…, well."

Remy shook harder. His voice wavered. "Yeah... I guess you're right." He tried hard to regain composure.

Rachiel reached across the island with her hand to hold her husband's hand.

"Rem, we'll be ok. I know we will. We'll figure this out."

Remy looked down and finally looked up into his wife's eyes. "Rach, how can you be sure?"

Rachiel squeezed her husband's hand and looked into his eyes as she leaned in closer. "Rem, I know we will. Hey, we're a team. Did you forget that? Whatever comes along, we'll figure it out!"

Remy looked back into his wife's eyes. "Rach, answer me, what did I ever do to deserve you?"

Rachiel smiled and stared at Remy. Her mind started wandering back to highlights of their relationship. She caught herself and stared into her husband's eyes.

"You didn't silly. We deserved each other. That's what happened! We made this together and we'll get through this together!"

Rachiel squeezed her husband's hands harder across the table.

Chapter 13

The work was hard, dirty, and taxing. Every day, Serafin shoveled coal seemingly endlessly from the piles in the railroad cars into the hoppers on the ships. Some days Serafin didn't finish until well into the night past the normal quitting time. When there were a lot of trains in use there was no time for rest. At times there were up to 6 ships waiting for coal bin fills. Serafin didn't complain though. It was honest work and paid him well. It also provided him with a solid source of self-esteem; his efforts were serving to ensure that the railroads ran. After all, if he didn't shovel the coal, the cities wouldn't have the raw ingredients to produce power which made them thrive.

Serafin waited for the bus late many nights, well past the time Bruno went home. But, every night that he arrived home he had dinner waiting for him. Bruno and his family treated Serafin as though he was a part of the family. And, when he arrived at the home of Bruno and Regina it was often Petrina who would serve him dinner. Many times when Serafin came home, the family was already gathered in the sitting room. They would read or listen to the radio every night after dinner and the chores. Serafin however, was so tired that he would sometimes just want to head to his room and lay down instead of joining them at the pastimes.

"So, Cornuto." Bruno called to Serafin from the other room as Serafin entered the house on a usual late night. Cornuto had turned into Serafin's name among the fellow railroad workers as started by Giuseppe. Seated in his chair, Bruno served to represent himself as the true king of the castle. On the small table next to him was the bottle of homemade red wine from his own garden. Accompanying that bottle was a glass half full of the contents of the aforementioned bottle. Serafin always smiled at the thought that Bruno's castle was a two story home on Central Avenue in Rochester, New York.

Serafin stopped in the foyer and as he was removing his wool overcoat answered, "Yes, Bruno?"

"You have been here 6 months. So, how do you like it here in America?"

Serafin didn't have to think hard about his reply as he hung up his coat. "Si, I like it."

75

Bruno lifted the glass to his lips and took a sip. "Ah, but all you do is work. You have to get out and see the city, enjoy the sights, get to know your environment."

Serafin made his way into the kitchen. Petrina was standing at the stove and warming his dinner. She smiled broadly at him, her smile saying silently "welcome home," as Serafin returned her smile. However, this wasn't the time for small talk, Bruno was interrogating Serafin.

Serafin answered: "I know, but, I haven't really had time. You told me that I had to work hard to gain favor and accomplish anything in this country."

Bruno smiled as he placed his glass down upon the small table near his chair.

"Yes, Yes I did. But, Serafin, you are missing something. A life of all work does not make a life. You have to enjoy the fruits of your labors, to, 'stop and smell the roses' like they say in this country. Tell me, I don't mean to get too personal, but what do you do with your money?"

Serafin entered the sitting room and stood close to the doorway.

'Well, I pay you for the room. And I buy my cigarettes. Some I send to mi Madre and, the rest, I save."

Bruno smiled and finally turned to the man he was questioning. "Save? Save for what?"

Serafin leaned against the door frame. "Well" Serafin stumbled a bit. "I appreciate all that you do for me, and the kindness that you have shown me. But… please, I don't mean any disrespect, but, I think I save for a place of my own."

Petrina dropped the Cornishware on the table and made an audible thump. She looked nervously first at Serafin and then at her Father.

Bruno turned away from Serafin and responded. "Ah, wise. But if you work and save all the time you will not have time to meet anyone. Will you?"

Even though Serafin was standing in the door entrance from the kitchen to the sitting room he felt Petrina's eyes on him. Petrina, meanwhile, was arranging Serafin's place setting while relegating her full attention to the conversation occurring.

"Si, you are right. But, I need to have enough to take care of that someone. What good is it to meet someone and not have the means to take care of them?"

Bruno laughed loudly and happily. "Serafin, you are right, but... If you wait for the right moment you may be waiting a long time. Life turns on a dime. Don't waste time waiting for the right time!"

Serafin smiled and thought deeply. Bruno had been a good friend to him and had yet to steer him wrong.

"Perhaps you are right, Il mi amico. Perhaps I will explore the city come this weekend."

Bruno answered with a smile in his voice. "Wise choice Serafin, now, mangia"

Serafin took his seat at the table that Petrina had prepared for him. He ate his meal and was once again, grateful for it. As he finished, he thanked Petrina and Regina for the wonderful meal. He then addressed himself to Bruno from the kitchen.

"Bruno, Gracias. Now, if you'll excuse me I will retire to my room. After all, I have to go to work in the morning"

Bruno answered without turning in his chair. "Bene, Serafin. Buonanotte."

"Buonanotte" Serafin replied.

"Scusi," Petrina said softly as though barely above a whisper. She had turned away from the sink and cautiously interrupted the conversation between her father and Serafin.

Serafin, hearing Petrina's voice, turned suddenly towards her direction. "Che?"

"Um... Well, if my father would allow me, I could show you the city"

Serafin smiled warmly at the pretty girl while glancing quickly in Bruno's direction. "That would be nice Petrina, but... you need to get permission from your father."

Bruno and Regina smiled. Of course, Bruno never turned in his chair. "Cornuto, normally I would say no. But... since it is you, perhaps my daughter has a point. After all, you would only get lost. And Petrina... well, she knows the city and I would be assured that you would make it back home."

Bruno grasped his chin with his hand. "In fact, I make you a deal. You accompany Petrina to the city for the weekly chores, perform all of our needs with our daughter and I will enjoy a day with my Regina."

Serafin chuckled aloud at Bruno's statement while Petrina smiled ear to ear and finished up washing the dishes.

Serafin addressed Bruno once again. "Of course, Bruno. I will do the family chores so that you may enjoy a day with Regina. It is the least that I could do for you, for the both of you!"

Petrina hurried over to the sofa and took up the knitting that she had left there.

"Then, it is settled. Buonanotte Serafin"

Serafin responded to all as he proceeded to the stairs. "Buonanotte....famiglia"

Serafin nodded to the family as he made his way up the stairs while Petrina, after cleaning the dishes, hurriedly rushed to sit happily on the sofa and picked up her knitting.

Chapter 14

The weeks wore on as Remy looked for work. Before that, he had been a good soldier and stayed with the company until the end as he was asked. As the other employees started splintering off and just started not showing up, Remy stuck it through. "You never know who will see this" Remy thought to himself. And, besides, he wasn't brought up that way. He was always taught to see a job through, no matter the outcome. A job was a responsibility and that is the way he treated it. Remy boxed and catalogued the files and papers for transport after they were through.

However, the reality was that Remy was still haunted by his feelings of guilt about the company closing. Although every fiber of his being told him that he wasn't at fault for the company's failure his inner voice told him otherwise. Have we, his generation, become so complacent that the efforts we put forward aren't what they could be because everything comes so easy compared to our forefathers. He couldn't help think of these things as he toiled to a losing cause. It was almost as if he was serving penance for the sin of a job not done properly before.

On the last day, Remy wandered the halls of the building for one last time. He stared down at the marble tiles that made up the floor, his eyes gathered in the deco-brick that adorned the walls. He suddenly realized how expensive and fine these were. The company had spared no expense when it built its testament to the corporate world. When clients and visitors entered the building the first thing they saw was the ornate decor and structure of the place. Like a pristine dressed executive the building served to intimidate any that would challenge her. However, whereas before the building represented the proud majesty of what the company wanted to stand for, now, in its emptiness, it paled in abject failure like a worn out Hollywood actress whose only sin was to grow old in an ever increasingly youth oriented industry always looking for the next best thing.

After the company officially closed its doors, the first thing Remy did was apply to the various job banks in the city. He dropped off a resume and filled out the appropriate paperwork with each job agency.

He then enrolled in the many online employment services, Careerblaster, Monstro, NationalJob and the like. He posted his resume and a cover letter on each sites' network. Remy then joined the networking sites such as LinkedIn. When he was working, he routinely ignored his co-worker's entreaties to join the social networking sites. Now, he began to question that logic. He also began to feel that his failure to join the sites actually hurt his job hunting efforts. "Well, this wasn't so bad" he thought, after finally signing up for the sites he had ignored once before.

Applying for unemployment didn't go quite as smoothly however. When he called the Unemployment office he was encouraged, no, literally required, to apply online. When he first signed up for his unemployment benefits he was told that he was not eligible immediately for the benefit. "What? this is impossible!" Remy thought nervously. He began pacing anxiously from his home office to the kitchen with the cordless phone. Every time he called the unemployment agency he got either a busy signal or hung up on. When he finally got through, it took 45 minutes of automated phone purgatory until he was finally connected to someone.

In the meantime, he had paced so often across the floor that he thought he was wearing a hole in the floor. He thought about the cartoons he used to watch as a kid and remembered when Fred Flintstone would pace so much he dug a trench into the floor. His thoughts raced continued to race incoherently and he purposely took off his slippers for fear that they were in actuality wearing down the carpet, which, he thought embarrassedly, he couldn't afford to replace at the moment.

Finally, a voice emerged from the other end of the phone.

"Hello, New York State Unemployment office, how can I help you?" the disinterested voice on the other end spoke. Remy was startled by the sudden break to his thoughts. He hesitated and stuttered as he attempted to regain his composure.

"Huh.. Hu..Hello, I'm..'m Remy Gayo, and I was trying to apply online for unemployment and it said that I wasn't eligible." He burst out the final words in his statement rapidly.

"Okay Mr. Gayo. Let me see if I can help you." The female voice on the other end answered indifferently, as though she had better things to do than bother with Remy.

After many agonizing minutes of giving her his Social Security number, former place of unemployment and the other impertinent information he was asked for, she returned with an answer.

"Well, Mr. Gayo, it appears that your company hasn't filed the appropriate paperwork on their end. Right now it is noted that you left your company with no cause. Therefore, unfortunately, as of this moment you are not eligible for unemployment benefits at this time."

The tone and matter-of-factness of her voice threw Remy for a loop. "That's not right! Don't you read the papers? The company claimed bankruptcy! None of us had a choice! We were all put out on the street without a job!"

The woman audibly sighed in contempt at Remy's outburst. "I understand that that is what you may think, Mr. Gayo, but, until the paperwork is filled out by your ex-employer, right now you are ineligible. You will have to wait the obligatory four to six weeks before you can start collecting. And, even then, that isn't guaranteed until after the results of the investigation."

Remy started to visibly shake. His heart rate increased and his forehead broke out in a sweat. He stood holding the phone to his ear while leaning on the kitchen island with his other arm. His face was turning red and his breath started coming rapidly. His voice went up an octave as he responded.

"Four to six weeks! What am I supposed to do until then!?"

The woman turned up her indifference level even higher. "Mr. Gayo, I can appreciate the fact that you are upset but it doesn't really serve any purpose to get upset at me. Now does it?"

Remy took a deep breath. Now she was quoting and using the "How to deal with irate callers" patented speeches. Remy had been through those seminars also, although they weren't really worth the paper they were printed on if the reader didn't believe in what they what was on the printed page.

Remy took a deep breath and attempted to compose himself. He smiled wickedly, what if he decided to play along, maybe he could get somewhere with this moron and perhaps even embarrass her. However, what she said next took him almost over the edge.

"Mr. Gayo, are you still there?"

Remy weakly responded, "Yes."

"While I'm sorry that I couldn't help you today, I will keep note on your file that you will be calling back. In the meantime, well, I'm sure you have some savings to tide you over. Don't you?"

Remy lost his composure again. "What do you mean by that? Are you saying that I didn't plan right? What the fuck was the purpose of the unemployment tax that was taken out of my check every week? So we can pay empathetic beauties like yourself?"

It took everything in Remy's power to not continue screaming at this woman. But, fortunately, logic settled into his mind, and he realized that he was getting nowhere with her. As he sat down at the kitchen island he began to regain composure and then, it hit him. Great, not only did the company make bad business decisions which cost him his job, but, they now handled the shut down poorly.

Remy took a deep breath and made a conscious effort to change the tone in his voice. "Look, I know it's not your problem. But, is there a supervisor or someone else I can talk to?"

This miffed the already taxed associate, "Look, I can try and find someone but they're going to tell you the same thing. I don't see why you won't take my word for it." The disdain was so evident in her voice it was if she was sitting next to Remy.

Remy caught the attitude in her voice and whether it was his anxiety or just his anger at her attitude he let loose. He had had enough of this game. "Let me tell you something. How would you feel if you were in my shoes? Huh?"

"Sir, there is no reason to get angry at me. I just work here"

"Yes, you're right. You JUST work there. Just like all the rest of the people in this country who "just work here" in their jobs. You know what's sad? What really is sad? It's the fact that most of us believe that! That we do "just work here" and therefore we only put the limited amount of effort in our jobs to get by! That's what's sad! Maybe if one or two of us treated our jobs as our livelihood things would be better!"

The woman on the other end was anxious to end this call. "Sir, if you continue in this badgering of me I will be forced to cease this call with you!"

Remy caught himself then, he began to realize the kind of person he was dealing with. "Yeah, I can tell. No wonder our government agencies perform as they do. Now, once again, can I speak to a supervisor?"

The voice sighed once again. "One moment, I'll see if I can locate one of the supervisors."

The wait was agonizingly long. But Remy refused to hang up. He was going to see this phone call through. While he was waiting for the supervisor he proceeded to make himself a cup of coffee. He also grabbed his laptop from his office and began to surf the web for jobs in the meantime. "I might as well make the most of my idle time" he thought. He again began to realize that perhaps he should have had that train of thought years ago.

After a wait of another twenty minutes a supervisor arrived on the phone. As Remy re-hashed his situation with her about half way into the conversation he realized that he was no better off. The supervisor essentially reiterated the prior conversation that he had with the first employee. The Supervisor, while appearing on the surface to be a bit more sympathetic than her employee, was still indifferent to Remy's plight. Remy realized that he was encountering people like he used to be. While he didn't picture himself as being as dismissive as they were, a small part of him questioned if he was like them. By this time Remy was tired and worn out.

As he hung up he resigned himself to log in every week and hope for a break. Otherwise he would have to use his savings. Hopefully, he would find a job by then.

Edward J. Indovina

Chapter 15

Saturday arrived and while Serafin didn't mind working hard, he was appreciative of having a day off. While the railroad still operated on the weekend Serafin had been placed on rotation with the other coal workers. He didn't mind working on Saturday, the money was good, but lately he just grew tired and looked forward to having a day off to recoup his thoughts and energy.

As the rays of light came through the sheer curtains of the window, Serafin decided to just lie in bed and enjoy the warmth of the sun. He smiled to himself and stretched out on the bed surface. The silence was pleasant for a change. The absence of the metallic clanging of the rail wheels, the steam engines, and the squeal of the metallic clasp brakes crying in agony as they tried in excruciating aspiration to bring nearly ten tons of iron and steel to a stop was sometimes so predominantly in his head it sometimes echoed during the off times.

His meditation was broken by the sound of the family rising. The squeaking of the wooden stairs leading downstairs betrayed its passengers as they filed down to the kitchen. Serafin arose, sat on the edge of his bed and proceeded to get ready for the day.

He made his way downstairs to join the family. Everyone was seated in their morning clothes except for Petrina. She was dressed and ready to go out with Serafin to perform the family chores. Bruno smiled as he bid Serafin good morning and glanced at Serafin and Petrina looking at each other.

Serafin couldn't take his eyes off of the suddenly pretty girl in front of him. He had never noticed the twinkling eyes or beautiful auburn hair of the girl whose house he had lived within for the last six months. It was as although a fog was lifted from his eyes and he realized what had been in front of him all this time.

He took his usual seat towards the middle of the table across from Petrina as Bruno sat at the foot of the table. Regina turned from the stove and served rolls and black coffee for Bruno and Serafin and coffee with warm milk for her girls.

Bruno broke the silence. "So, Serafin. Today you run commissioni. Lo sono riconoscente."

Serafin smiled and replied to Bruno. "Il suo nulla, after all that you have done for me, it is the least that I can do."

Bruno leaned back in his chair, elevating the front legs off the floor and brought his coffee to his lips. "Si, but it is not necessary to repay me. You have earned everything on your own with your character and work ethic. After all, haven't I taught you anything? If we cannot help each other, what else is there?"

Serafin smiled towards Bruno. "Capisco, Bruno"

Bruno settled the chair down to the surface and placed both of his hands on the table. "It will be a good day for me. I am going to get a head start on the garden and take care of the little things around the house."

Regina smirked and announced loudly from her vantage point of the stove. "Yes, by two he will be snoring in his chair in the garden with that awful smelling De Nobili cigar burning between his sleeping fingers! And, that will be after he gets done announcing repeatedly "Regina, amore mio, mi volete prendere un panino! Then, he will ask me for a glass of lemonade while he stares at his garden! Not tend it!"

The girls broke out laughing. Apparently this was a pattern of Bruno's that Serafin hadn't seen yet. Bruno sat there nonplussed, though Serafin could detect a slight grin on his face.

Petrina leaped up from her chair with a spirited conviction to change the subject. "And I will make sure that Serafin comes home with everything we need papa!"

Bruno smiled warily, "Yes, I'm sure you will. Now, Cornuto, you are to keep an eye on my little girl. If anything should happen to my little flower there will be hell to pay!"

Serafin rocked back a little, "Bruno, rest assured, I will watch over her as though she were my own!"

Petrina stood over her father playfully defiant. "Papa! I am almost sixteen; I know how to take care of myself! I am a woman you know!"

Bruno smiled ear to ear and grasped his daughter's hand. "Si, si. I know my little Petrina, but, you have to understand. You will always be my little Petrina, no matter how old you become!"

Serafin sat and smiled at the Father and his daughter. "Petrina, you cannot fault your father for looking after you. You are lucky to have a father that loves you that much."

Petrina pouted slightly. But her disposition remained for only a few seconds as she thought of her day ahead. As the family finished breakfast Petrina rushed to clear the table and clean the dishes. Serafin in the meantime went up to his room to dress to leave.

Chapter 16

The weeks dragged on for Remy. He got to the point of checking his e-mail at least six times a day. Sure, he got offers, but they were all cyber-marketing offers. Jobs with self-starter, great income potential, and other such 'buzz' words attached. As Remy dug into the companies he found that most of the jobs were no security, no guarantee, type of positions. Most of them entailed cold calling sales and products that no one wanted or could particularly afford in the current economic climate.

Remy's bit of good news during this period was that the unemployment benefit situation was finally resolved and he received a lump sum in retroactive benefits. The lump sum went quite a ways to take care of the bills for the month, but as Remy sat down, he began to realize that what he was receiving in unemployment benefits wouldn't be enough to cover the bills for the next month.

He began to get a little nervous. His mind was constantly occupied with that fact and it was affecting his well-being. He had to get it off his chest and waited one night until the kids were in bed and Rachiel and he were alone.

Remy sat at the kitchen island nervously fidgeting with a glass of wine and his biscotti. As long as Remy could remember this was a little ritual that Rachiel and he had settled into. Even before the kids were born Remy and Rachiel used to wind down the day with their ritual of wine and a cookie.

"Rach, I'm getting a little nervous."

Rachiel looked at her husband. "About what, honey?"

"This job thing. It's not coming together."

Rachiel tried to sound optimistic for her husband. "Rem, it's going to take time."

Remy visibly sighed and his shoulders slumped. His eyes glanced down with defeat. "Rach, how much time is enough time? I mean, how long is it going to take?"

"Rem, look, I can't tell you for certain, but these things take time. All good things take time. I've been picking up extra hours at the store, so I can help"

Remy sighed deeply and looked down at the table trying to maintain his composure in front of his wife. He didn't have the courage to tell her that in his heart of hearts he felt that she wasn't doing enough. He really knew that it wasn't the case, but he couldn't help but feel that way. Yet, if he really examined his feelings, he knew that he would realize that he, himself, created this position.

When things were well, he actually discouraged his wife from taking a full time job. His mother didn't work full time and he didn't want his wife to do so. After all, wasn't that the way things were supposed to be?

"Rach, I know you're trying. But the extra hours isn't really going to do that much for us."

Rachiel sensed her husband's demeanor and fought back her own tendency to combat this line of reasoning. She was wise enough to know that this was neither the time, nor the place, to challenge the conversation. "Remy, How do you figure that? Doesn't every little bit help?"

Remy took a deep breath, sipped his wine and addressed his wife. "Rach, our mortgage on this house is over $1000. Then, take into account our food, insurance, car payment, heat, electric, telephone, and the rest of the miscellaneous expenses. Now, while I'm getting the maximum from unemployment, it's still only $400 a week. We're stuck. Need I go on?"

It finally began to hit Rachiel. Whereas before, she figured if she remained calm she could help them weather this storm. Now, the reality of the situation was hitting her. She didn't realize that it would take this long for Remy to find work. Actually, she couldn't remember a time when he didn't have a job. It just had seemed like he was always there, working and providing for them. Now, it was incomprehensible, Remy not working.

Her thoughts started to turn gray also. Was it her fault? Was it their fault? Should they have planned better? Then again, who could have foreseen this? But, was that the real issue? Did they become so dependent on the length of their good fortune that they lost the drive they initially had when they were young and struggling? Were they that foolish that they didn't take into account the normal ups and downs of life itself?

Rachiel started to tear up. She knew it was tough but she figured they could tough it out.

She caught herself in her composure and spoke to Remy. "Rem, come on, we can do it. How about some of your old business acquaintances? Have you called any of them for help?"

"No, I haven't. Do you think it would do any good? I mean, they all know I'm out of a job, don't you think if they needed someone they would call me?"

Rachiel smirked to herself. Her gray thoughts were playing out in reality. Perhaps her feelings were right. "Rem, the world doesn't come to you. You have to go to it. Remember what daddy used to say?"

Remy shook his head. Just the mere mention of his father-in-law still served to send fear in him. Actually, Remy respected his father-in-law greatly, it just seemed as though he never stopped pushing Remy.

"Rach, your dad is a pretty colorful guy. He says a lot of things."

"Yes, he does. But what he does say makes sense in some situations."

Remy sat in silence as he finished his wine. He could almost hear Salvatore's and his father's voice in his head. "Nothing worthwhile falls into your lap; everything comes with sweat, and occasionally tears. If you want something you have to work towards it!"

Remy took a deep breath, he was anxious to end this trip down memory lane and his feelings of discontent towards his wife. "You're right Rach. I will, tomorrow. Now, let's go to bed. After all, I have to get up in the morning to start working at getting work."

As he rose from his chair he stood and presented his outstretched hand for Rachiel to join him. They proceeded up the stairs to their bedroom leaving the glasses on the island.

Chapter 17

Serafin continued to work hard and do well in his job. He had begun to save a bit of money and life felt a bit easier. The complete hospitality of the Santagelos was almost numbing to him. How people could be so kind made him feel as though he were home and one of the family.

Petrina, meanwhile, had clearly taken a shine to their border and her parents didn't object. She had just celebrated her 16th birthday and was starting to blossom into a beautiful woman.

Serafin was a fine, hard working young man and carried himself well also. His self confidence grew as he became more comfortable in his job and with the increasing amount of savings he was starting to amass. The knowledge that he could take care of himself also helped to lend a confidence to his feelings. Everything worked symbiotically, hard work leads to earnings, leads to a roof over one's head, which, in turn, leads to self-confidence.

In the meanwhile, he had begun to help with the chores and tasks around the Santagelo's home without being asked. So much so, that, in fact, he had begun to be treated as family and not as just a border. It became a regular occurrence in the city for Petrina and Serafin to perform the shopping duties for the family on a regular basis. Many of the merchants had begun to comment on what a fine young couple that the two of them were and mentioned the fact to Regina and Bruno whenever they saw them.

One Saturday, as they walked the Main Street of the city leaving Gino the baker and heading over to Mario the Butcher, Serafin asked Petrina a question.

"So, what do you want to do with your life? You are almost a woman now and you are almost out of school."

Petrina looked up at Serafin a little disconcertedly. "Um, I have never really thought about it, Seri."

Serafin realized he had made Petrina nervous, and, that was the last thing he would ever want to do to her. He consciously lightened the tone of his inquiry. "Piccolo, non volevo turbati. Ero solo curioso."

Petrina understood her slight overreaction; it was just that Serafin made her nervous sometimes. She was fearful of answering him the wrong way at times. She thought more of him than she cared to let on.

"I understand, ho capito. I just, I guess I hadn't really thought of it yet."

"Si, si. I know, perdonami, mi Petrina. I was just curious. You are very intelligent and so adept with your hands. I just wondered if you thought of the future at all."

As they walked down the crowded street Petrina moved to avoid bumping into a fellow pedestrian. As she did so, her hand brushed Serafin's.

Petrina turned flush with nervousness. "Scusi…"

Serafin smiled and took hold of Petrina's hand as they made their way through the crowd. "There is no need to be shy, mi Petrina. After all, I promised your Padre I would make sure nothing happened to you. So, I will keep you close."

Petrina looked up at Serafin as they walked towards Mario's.

"Ah, the young couple! Benvenuto!" Mario yelled from behind the counter as Serafin and Petrina entered his shop. Petrina consciously let go of Serafin's hand as they entered the shop.

Mario's butcher shop was like most shops of the time. The front window featured hanging slabs of meat on display to entice the shopper to enter. Once inside, the wooden plank floors were covered with sawdust and the exterior shelves were stocked with various types of olive oils and spices. Cured meats and sausages were hanging from the ceiling in their nets and cheesecloth to catch any remaining drippings. However, the true action took place behind the counter.

As the crowd in front of the counter shouted out their orders, Mario and his helper were like acrobats. They would retrieve the slabs of carcass and carve out the requested orders for the patrons. So deft they were with their knives that nothing went to waste. Long cuts of fat and rough trims were saved in a bucket for future use as suet and ground cuts.

Being immigrants in America, many of Mario's customers were not accustomed to such nice cuts of beef and pork. In their native lands they were relegated to creating and eating recipes built around the cuts of the animals that were made available to them.

The cheap cuts of meat were usually slow cooked in liquids and sauces to enhance their palatability. More times than not, there was no meat available and it was usually just rice, beans, or polenta that they made out of corn meal. The only ones that were able to enjoy loin and fine cuts in their native lands were the nobility. Otherwise, fowl, hare, and wild game were the meats of choice by the more resourceful. To have a shop like Mario's available to them only served to enforce the perception that America was truly the promised and blessed land.

"Petrina! Serafin! Come Stai!"

"Molte bene, Grazie!" Petrina answered Mario. Serafin nodded his head towards Mario.

"The usual, right?" Mario indicated as he began to prepare the packages for them. Petrina nodded in agreement to Mario's initial question.

Mario spoke to Petrina as he prepared the Santangelo's order. "So, how are your mother and father?"

Petrina smiled appreciatively at Mario's inquiry. "Bene, bene. Thank you for asking."

"Ah, your i genitori are fine people." He handed a box full of brown paper wrapped cuts of meat over the counter to Serafin.

"Say hello to them for me!"

"Si, I will. Thank you again." Petrina handed Mario an envelope.

"Che cosa e questo? Payment isn't due till the end of the month."

Petrina nodded as she began to turn towards the shop door. "Si, mio padre knows that. He told me to pay you now. He wanted you to know that he appreciated your patience when he was late and would like to make it up to you."

Mario went flush in the face with gratitude. "Grazie, grazie. Your father is a good man." Mario quickly shoved the envelope in his pocket and turned to start helping another customer.

Petrina and Serafin nodded goodbye and made their way out of the shop back to the street. The two of them visited numerous other shops over the span of the next few hours.

After they had finished the shopping for the day they made their way home by hopping on the back of an open body stake truck with their packages as the driver waved them on. The truck slowed in front of the house and as they bid thank you to the driver they entered the home laden with packages.

Regina greeted them at the door and relieved her daughter of some of her burden. "Bene, did you get everything?" Regina asked as she placed the boxes on the countertop.

Petrina answered confidently towards her mother. "Si, Madre. Everything. Mario sends his best wishes."

"Good, he is a good man." Regina nodded approvingly.

Serafin had begun to help the ladies empty the boxes of goods. Regina placed her hand on Serafin's arm to stop him.

"Aspettare, Serafin. Relax, you have done enough. The girls and I will unpack those. You relax and rest a little."

Serafin nodded. "Grazie, Regina. So, where is Bruno?"

Regina continued emptying the boxes and snidely replied. "Where do you think? The big 'worker' is out in his garden asleep with his wine and cigar!" Regina laughed aloud.

Serafin nodded, thought quickly and replied to Regina and Petrina. "Ok, I go to my room now to write to my mother. Ciao!"

Serafin had begun to write to his mother and brothers on a regular basis at the insistence of Regina and Petrina. Their encouragement was based on two emotions, empathy, and curiosity about Serafin's background. Regina knew that the young man had been brought up proper and right since it was reflected in his proper manners and courtesies.

Regina, as a mother herself, could almost feel what Serafin's mother felt with the absence of her youngest son. She knew that it had to be excruciating to have ambivalent thoughts about the well-being of one of the loves of her life. A letter, even though it took up to two weeks to arrive, would at least give a mother at least one peaceful night's sleep knowing that her son was all right for the moment she read the letter until the next morning when she would start worrying again.

One night, after Serafin and Bruno had arrived from work, Serafin opened his mail as he sat at the table with Regina and Petrina. Serafin read one letter and visibly became excited. "Fantastico, Gracias a Dios en el cielo!"

Regina smiled and queried Serafin, she had never seen this much emotion in their young border before. "Che? What is the news Serafin?"

Serafin embarrassedly realized how he had looked to the women. "Lo siento mucho! Pero yo no puedo creer las noticias! Estoy muy orgullosa de él!"

He caught himself, he was speaking in his native tongue. He apologized to his hosts. "Mi scusi, but my brother has been accepted into the priesthood! I am so happy for him!"

Regina answered first. "Why, that's wonderful! You must be very proud of him!"

Serafin smiled visibly excited and proud for his brother and family. "Si, Si. It is a wonderful thing. Now my family has two priests! We are very blessed."

Regina looked at Serafin quizzically. Never once did he mention that there were priests in his family, nor that he was so religious. In fact, even when they attended church on Sundays, Serafin never seemed to incline a mastery of his faith beyond his attendance.

Regina was intrigued with this new revelation of her border turned pseudo-son though. "So, your other brother is a priest also?"

"Si, in fact..." he trailed off.

"What, Serafin?"

Serafin regained composure of his facial expression. "Niente. I am very proud of my brother."

Regina and Petrina sensed perhaps a slight sadness in him. Regina was content to retract her line of questioning, but it was Petrina now who pressed the issue. "Seri, what is it? Why didn't you finish your thought?"

Seri was Petrina's pet name for Serafin when they were out. This was the first time she had used it in front of her family. They all looked at Petrina and then Serafin. Even Bruno craned an ear towards the table. After all, this was the first time that Serafin had ever come close to talking about his family.

"Eh, no matter, it is done now"

"What is done? What?" Petrina pressed hard now.

"Well, I'm sure you don't want to hear about me. How was your day?"

Regina and Petrina laughed at Serafin's stall tactic. Petrina looked sternly at Serafin from across the table. "Don't you dare, Signore Gayo. Tell us."

Serafin looked helplessly towards Bruno in the other room. But Bruno adjusted himself in his chair and shook his head as if saying, "You're in it now."

Serafin had no choice but to respond. "Well..." Serafin started slowly.

"Mia Madre e mio padre had three sons. When I was about nine years old my father passed away and my mother raised myself and my brothers by herself. She is a strong woman; she worked cleaning others' clothes and performing their tailoring. Sometimes, when we didn't have enough to eat she would feed us boys while she sat there working. She would sit there on her sewing stool and work while she watched and made sure that we ate enough at the table. Even though I was young it pained me to see her go hungry but you could not argue with her. She would get very angry if we did not eat and threatened us with the orfanotrofio or the switch if we didn't obey her. On Sundays we would walk to the village and go to church. After mass we would perform chores around the Canonica. Little things, like weed the landscaping, wash the windows, carry water, and other small items while my Mother would clean the floors and the vestibules."

Serafin took a breath and rambled on. "Afterwards we would have dinner with the priests and then we would retreat for home. It was the one day of the week where my Mother didn't have to worry about where dinner was coming from. Although she worked on that day cleaning, She would tell me when I got older that it was actually a day of rest for her because it was the one day she didn't have to fret about our well-being."

Everyone's eyes were fixated upon Serafin as he continued. He continued staring to the side, not particularly looking at anyone in particular as he spoke.

"Well, I guess you could say that we were practically brought up in the church and mio fratello Maggiore signed up for the Seminario. After he did, my other brother followed. It was expected that I would do the same, but..." He paused. "But, I... just thought that there was something more. Something more than what I could get out of the church, or the country."

"Vedo che..." Regina muttered.

"Per favore, I mean no.. mancanza di rispetto towards my mama. But... with the rise of the Spanish foreign legion, there was no other way for me to stay in Spagna. If I didn't go to the Seminario, I would be forced into the army. And, quite frankly, that, that I just didn't want to do. A man shouldn't be forced to "serve a cause in which his heart is not into."

The family was silent for a moment, and then Petrina broke the silence. "Seri, we are very glad you chose to bless us with yourself. The Lord has brought you to us and us to you. Now, enough melancholy, enjoy what we and yourself have, if not by ourselves, then together!"

She slapped the top of the wooden table which jolted Serafin and his head jumped back.

"Madre de Dios! Petrina! Where did the thunder come from in you!" he exclaimed.

With that, everyone broke out laughing loudly. Bruno laughed so hard he shook the chair.

Bruno then commanded, "Si, now chiudere! I want to listen to the new radio that I bought!"

Serafin bellowed in response, "Si, you bought, I carried home from the shop!"

Bruno laughed again, "You are young, strong, and willing to anything to help, eh? Well, you did. You brought us a radio!"

Everyone took a seat in the sitting room and listened. Serafin gazed at Petrina and smiled broadly. He definitely looked at her in a new light and, was more attracted than ever before to her.

Edward J. Indovina

<u>Chapter 18</u>

Remy began the day with a new found purpose and a lift in his step. His talk with Rachiel the night before had served to fire him up. While he didn't sleep fitfully, his lack of sleep served to have him replay their conversation from the night before in his head. He arose from their King size bed and took a shower immediately in their adjoining shower. He dressed in business casual attire and headed down the stairs. He paused and looked around at his bedroom surroundings. He was blessed, he realized, and he had much more than others did. Now, it was time for him to work hard to keep it. As he entered the kitchen area Sari, Angela, and Rachiel all stared at him. Remy smiled at his family and sat himself at the dining room table. As he took his place at the table he took a notepad and comprised a list of people he would call today. They were all business associates he had befriended over the years. If he was going to network he would network his immediate contacts first.

Remy bid his family off to their days. He gave a quick kiss on the cheek to Sari and Angela and when Rachiel left he gave his beautiful wife a kiss on the lips.

"Well, you seem quite alive today"

"Rach, I told you, that talk last night struck a chord with me. You're absolutely right; the world doesn't come to me."

After his family had left he set himself up in his home office. He grabbed the cordless phone from the kitchen and opened up his contact book. Rachiel and the kids would make fun of him because he kept a paper phone book instead of using his cellular phone or his PC for his contacts. No, he kept a paper book just like his Father did. While Remy lived in the 21st century he didn't always embrace the modern technologies like many of his peers. Sometimes he preferred the old methods that his father and grandfather used. However, in actuality, he was afraid to admit aloud, that he thought that the technology made people indifferent and removed from everyday life.

He began his day by calling his friend Mark Castrile. Mark was a purchasing manger over at Sullivan Electronics. Remy had known Mark for years and, while they had never spent physical time together, Remy considered him a friend.

Remy listened to the phone ringing on the other end as he rehearsed his conversation in his head. His thoughts were broken by the sound of Mark's voice.

"Hello, thank you for calling Sullivan Electronics, Mark here."

Remy paused with nervous anxiety and quickly regained his composure. "Mark? Hi, it's me, Remy. Remy Gayo."

"Oh, hey. Hi Remy, how you been?"

"Ok, I guess. How's it going with you?"

"Well, you know. The same old. Well, actually, been working a bit harder. They reduced our support staff and laid more on those of who are left." Mark answered tiredly.

Remy replied sympathetically, "Wow, that's rough."

Mark realized that he was sounding negative and attempted to change gears. "How's it going with you?"

Remy replied, "Well, I'm sure you heard. They shut the place down"

Mark audibly sighed. He had known that, he just didn't want to bring it up. He felt uneasy talking about it with Remy. Actually, he couldn't bear to think of what it would feel like if he lost his job.

"Ummm, yeah, I thought I heard something like that. How you doing?"

Remy could sense Mark's discomfort. "Not good. Can't find a job. Anything by you?"

Mark paused..."Umm. Gee, I don't know. I'll ask around. But, you know how it is. They cut our staff here."

Remy sighed loudly. "Yeah, I get the picture." He knew by Mark's actions there was no chance in Mark asking anyone. Actually, he sensed that Mark was concerned about his own well being and the last thing Mark wanted was for his own livelihood to be in jeopardy by helping another.

Mark answered lightly. "Hey, don't get down. I know something'll come up. I will ask around. I promise" Mark started to feel Remy's desperation through the phone.

Remy knew a lost cause when he heard one. "Thanks, well, thanks for listening to me, Mark."

"Rem, anytime, and..." his voice raising "I will ask, I mean it."

Remy knew that it was Mark's selfish guilt answering that, not himself. "Thanks, Thanks a lot. I'll see you."

Remy put the phone down on his desk and shook his head. Although he felt dejected, he took a deep breath and shook off the disappointment. After all, what did he expect? Success on the first call that he made? He made another phone call to another contact on his list. However, with each ensuing call it was more of the same. Businesses were withholding hiring due to the current economic and government climate. As the economy turned downward the new administration in the federal government was beginning to pass more and more legislation in and effort 'assist' the national economy. Additionally, the government began passing more regulation to generate income to make up for the lost tax income that began to occur. Yet, despite all of the Feds 'assistance' Remy didn't feel it, in fact, all he felt was more helplessness.

Remy decided to take a drive to shake off what he was feeling. He kept telling himself that it would all come together, that these things take time. He thought of Rachiel and the kids to ground him. He spotted a pizza shop and decided to get lunch there.

As he walked in, he went up to the counter and ordered two slices of pizza and an iced tea. Taking a glance around him, he saw people of all walks of life. In the Pizzeria there were business people in shirts and ties, students, older people, and regular working class individuals enjoying their lunch.

As he finished his lunch the anxiety began to hit him again. How was he going to pay the bills? How was he going to feed his family? He looked around furtively in the restaurant and talked himself down. He threw a tip on the table and got up to leave.

Looking around he noticed that it was rare for people in this pizzeria to leave a tip. Remy, although he really didn't have the change to spare, couldn't justify to himself to not leave a tip. These poor people had it worse than he did, he felt, and they were working!

He left the pizzeria and got into his car. As he continued driving he came to a decision. "I've put enough into the system all these years. Shouldn't I be able to use the system now until I get back on my feet?" It took a lot for Remy to swallow his pride but he made his decision. He pulled into the Social Services headquarters parking lot, took a deep breath and headed in.

This was the first time in his life that he had ever been in a place like this. As he entered through the glass doors he approached the information desk. In a way, the lobby resembled the lobby of his old employer. It was a spacious, open lobby with elevators to the left and hallways and offices toward the rear. He stopped at the desk and the young girl disinterestedly looked up at him while still maintaining a downward glance at her cell phone.

"Can I help you?" she replied as her eyes turned back down towards her phone.

"Yes, um... I would like to apply for.. Public assistance." the words came out of Remy's mouth as though they caused him pain. He glanced furtively around as he said them and then looked at the girl.

"Yes, that's what we do here." she answered while typing on her phone.

Remy snapped into reality. He asked the blasé girl. "Ok, well.., where do I go?"

The young girl stopped her typing and responded annoyed and indifferently. "Back there. Room three," she pointed over her shoulder towards the rear hall. "Here, fill this out, give it to the aide and you'll be called when they're ready for you."

She handed Remy a booklet and a pencil. In the meantime she resumed her typing and continued while the phone next to her rang incessantly.

"Cripes" Remy thought. She couldn't be more than 23 and yet she could care less about her job. Just to have the audacity to use her cell phone at work blew Remy away. She was worse than the receptionist they had at Suncoast. No, she was much worse; actually, she didn't have a single bit of acceptable social grace.

Remy made his way down the hall towards offices. It was there when he encountered an enlightening moment. As he made his way down the hall he suddenly had a thought that he had entered another dimension. While he expected to find poor, destitute people like that were shown on television, the reality of the situation set him back. He took a seat along the wall and began to fill out the booklet. As he looked around as he filled in the answers to the questions and took in the atmosphere of where he sat.

Instead of likeable hobos and women with layers of unmatched cast off clothing that were shown in the movies, there were the diametric opposite within this building. Seated in the waiting areas were people of all ethnicities and ilk. Instead of the stereotypical tattered coats and disheveled hair, the occupants sat in their new coats, designer hats, freshly manicured nails, designer bags for the women, designer shoes for the men and pristine hairdos.

Also, instead of everyone being gaunt and famished, they were loud, obnoxious, demanding, and, for the most part, at least in Remy's eyes, abhorrently overweight. In addition, the scene within the building was resolute chaos. There were children screaming, running around, with no apparent effort upon the parents to quell their children's' rambunctiousness and disruptiveness. On top of all that, Remy thought, there were children who had children. And, these children were no older than Sari or Angela. Even more shockingly, in Remy's mind, was that no one was thankful or ashamed for the benefits they were asking for or receiving already. They carried themselves as though this was their right, what was owed to them.

Remy turned in his paperwork and sat back down. As he sat outside of room 3, Remy began to feel self-conscious about his appearance. He didn't have long to remain in that state of mind, thankfully.

"Mr. Gayo!"

Remy stood up at the announcement of his name. He entered the room and looked at the origin of the voice.

"This way sir" The aide pointed Remy towards the consultation room in much the same manner and attitude as the front receptionist. She also appeared to be about the same age and social strata of the girl at the front desk.

Remy walked in and took a seat in front of the social worker. Remy noticed that the chair was leather, with inset brass tacks holding the leather onto the frame. The desk in front of the chair was made of cherry wood and ornately cut. On the surface of the desk was a padded desk mat. To the right of Remy, on top of the desk, was a small American flag and to the left was a brass pen and pencil holder.

The woman seated at the desk appeared to be approximately middle-aged, well dressed, perhaps African-American, and confidently self-assured. Although seated, her average build was evident in the way her sport coat hung from her slim shoulders and blouse opened up at the top buttons. While she did not come from a middle-class home, she embraced her present position in life and carried herself as though she were royalty. It was obvious that she envisioned herself in a much higher social position than what she actually was. A collegiate degree, in her mind, allowed her more courtesies than other, less driven people or, fortunate people in the world. Her diplomas and accreditations were displayed proudly on the walls of the office. While she was quite pleased with her accomplishments, she failed to realize that she lived in a fortunate time where she was able to obtain the resources in order to achieve her higher education.

Without looking up she started her speech directed towards Remy. "Mr. Gayo, my name is Wanda McNeilson, in going over your application I am afraid I have to advise you that currently you are not eligible for the benefits you have applied for at this time."

Remy rocked back a little and started to shake. Whilst he had anticipated this answer, it still shook him. "What do you mean?"

Still, without looking up, she continued. "Well, your income is too high and you have many resources that can be applied to your situation that haven't been used yet."

Remy swallowed hard, he had started to shake although he fought to maintain his composure. He took a deep, visible breath as he answered. "What resources? And, what income? I listed my expenses; I'm going to be short paying them!"

The woman finally looked up at Remy. Her gaze and demeanor registered contempt as she delivered her answer. "Mr. Gayo, as much we would like to help you. The guidelines are the guidelines. And, right now, you have too much."

Remy looked at her incredulously. "Too much! How is it too much! I'm getting $400 a week from unemployment and my expenses are over $3000." he replied alarmed.

Ms. McNeilson averted her gaze from Remy's eyes. "Mr. Gayo, please. I don't react well to excitement."

Remy caught his breath.

"Ms. McNeilson, I have worked for more than 18 years for the same firm. Every pay check close to 30% is removed for the various state and local taxes that I, as a working citizen, am required to pay. Now, mind you, I have never once have I complained or shirked from that responsibility. However, I was under the impression, I now realize mistakenly, that those taxes were to assist me and my family in cases of misfortune. "

Ms. McNeilson once again looked up at Remy. "Mr. Gayo..."

Remy cut her off and continued. "I was under the impression that as an American I paid those taxes so that we, as a country, can help those that need it. That everyone has bad times sometimes and we all need help in those times. Instead, what I see is a system that has been bastardized and turned into a perpetual cycle where the same people use it over and over instead of occasionally, as it was set up to be. Or, obviously, those same taxes go to pay for nice offices, salaries, and educations of people whom the federal government have deemed proper due to their heritage and ancestry. It's wrong, period. And, I also see, that the people who truly need it, like myself, can't get it because we did the right things all of our lives. Is that fair?"

McNeilson looked at Remy disgustedly and sighed audibly. "Mr. Gayo. I can appreciate your frustration. However, your 401K and your savings account are too much to be considered. Perhaps, and I'm just speaking theoretically of course, if you transferred those accounts to your children or a relative you could obtain help. But then, there is the matter of your home..."

Remy was taken aback once again. Did he just hear what he thought he heard? Lie about your assets? The fruits of your hard work labors? The things he was told to do to ensure his future? "This is fucked" he thought.

"Do you mean to tell me that because I worked hard, saved my money and planned for the future by living in my means that I'm penalized?"

"Mr. Gayo, I am only telling you the rules."

Remy smirked visibly and chuckled softly, yet nastily. He knew he had no choice with these people so he decided in his mind to go for broke with his next statement.

"The Rules! FUCK your rules! Out in those hallways are people who are perfectly capable of working for a living but they choose not to because it's too easy for them to collect for free. I see parents, their children, and their children's children all lined up to collect what is truly not theirs. They have figured out the system and have passed it down to the next ones. Do you know what I drove here? A Saturn. A SATURN! It looks awful crappy next to the Escalades, Mercedes, BMWs, and Cadillacs in that parking lot. And then, then you have the audacity to tell me to hide my assets so that I can get benefits. Well, you know what? I'll be damned if I'm going to lie to get what is entitled to me! And, you. You are a real piece of work. You sit there with your better-than-thou attitude in your department store clothing with your Saltaa makeup and you look down on me. Why? Because I appear privileged to your twisted mind? Do you think that because you earned a degree entitles you to be better than me? Well, the jokes on you. Just because I don't have a fancy degree doesn't mean that I don't know what hard work is. My grandfather had to work hard to achieve what he had also when he came here. And, my Father wasn't allowed to pursue higher education. His family couldn't afford it. Did you pay for your education? I doubt it? Your attitude repulses me! The system needs to be changed. And changed now!"

Ms. McNeilson just sat there staring contemptuously at Remy. "Mr. Gayo. I am sorry you feel the way that you do, and quite frankly, I am offended by your insinuations. It doesn't matter how I achieved my accreditations, it is a testament to myself that I did!"

"How dare me? How dare you? You're nothing but a …" Remy caught himself. It wouldn't serve his purpose to engage in a pointless debate with someone of such beliefs. He smiled to himself. It wasn't her fault he thought. She was a part of Remy's generation that took no blame or responsibility for their actions. It was their God-given right to not have to struggle to achieve anything,

"Mr. Gayo, I see by the smirk on your face something I have said proved to amuse you, but, in regard to your request, the rules are the rules."

"Yeah, I figured that out. You know what I find funny? Is that many of the people out there are immigrants like my grandfather and my wife's father. However, do you know what? I don't ever remember stories of them going to the government for benefits. In fact, all I remember is stories about how when things got tough they worked harder. Not run for a handout!"

"Mr. Gayo, I believe we are done for the day. Unless you can change your attitude."

Remy smirked again and came to a determination.

"Well, Ms. McNeilson. Rest assured, this will be the first and last time I meet with you on this platform. The next time you hear from me will not be conducive to your position. I feel comfortable letting you know that I will do everything I can to become a thorn in your side"

McNeilson shook her head in silence as Remy walked out and Remy felt ashamed at the words he had spoken towards her. He reminded himself again that her attitude was learned and not experienced.

Edward J. Indovina

Chapter 19

Serafin, while everything was going fine for him, was starting to feel restless. He had saved up a considerable amount of money and was feeling the itch to have a place of his own. His time with the Santangelo family had been a true blessing. And Serafin had tried to contribute but he had always felt as though it wasn't enough. He had an uneasy feeling that he was beginning to overstay his welcome. On top of all of this, there was the matter of Petrina.

It was no secret that he had become enamored with the girl and her, in turn, with him. He fought to recognize her as nothing more than a sister. Yet, that wasn't the truth. He was a boarder and she was the landlord's daughter. Serafin had deep feelings for the girl / woman. As Serafin thought about it, he realized, he felt guilty as though he was betraying the kindness of Bruno and Regina, but he couldn't help but keep thinking about Petrina.

Bruno and his fellow workers had shown him how things work in this country. You take your opportunities as they come and you don't squander them. Here, when Serafin arrived, Bruno gave him a room to stay. Then, Giuseppe offered him a job so that he could earn his way. The secret to all of these opportunities were that none of them were given gratis. Each opportunity had a cost attached to them. Whether it was a room, job, or meals, they all took a payment of either monetary or personal labor. And, even the monetary value only came with personal labor. Every opportunity was earned and the breadth of the value of the opportunity was in direct relation to the amount of effort that was put into it. Serafin grew to appreciate and love his new country and displaced, adopted, countrymen.

Similarly, he grew to appreciate and love Petrina. It was if, every day he noticed something new and exciting about the young woman. She was smart, caring, talented, and ambitious, all the qualities of his own mother. Petrina knew her way around a book as much as she knew her way around a kitchen.

Serafin approached Bruno on a Saturday afternoon. He was apprehensive to approach this subject matter. During that day, Serafin had completed the family chores with Petrina and when they arrived home Bruno was out in the garden.

After he had delivered the packages to Regina, Serafin went out into the backyard to join Bruno. "Ciao, Bruno,"

Bruno looked up with a start. He had been dozing in the sunlight amongst his grape vines with a glass of wine and his cigar. "Oh, Ciao Serafin. Come ha fatto andare tutto oggi?"

"Fine, Fine, Bruno. Petrina is helping Regina and Verotta are putting the items away now. Oh, by the way, Mario the butcher sends his blessings once again."

Bruno was seated in one of the two fabric mesh wooden framed chairs that he had in the garden. He motioned for Serafin to join him.

"Sedersi. I am sure you didn't come out here to talk to me about Mario. Tell me, what's on your mind? I can sense that you have an ulterior motive to meeting me out here, cornuto."

Serafin smiled , Bruno had a extra sense to know whenever something was bothering one of his family or Serafin, whom by now, he considered family.

Actually he had that sense with most everyone. At work, many of the employees sought out Bruno for his wisdom and advice. Even Giuseppe treated Bruno more like a father figure than an employee. Bruno's nickname at the railroad was Padre Saggio, Wise Father. Of course, Bruno didn't quite like that name. It made him feel old, even though he was older than most of the men at the Railroad, he didn't like to consider himself as such.

"Grazie. Bruno, you know that I have a great deal of rispetto per voi."

Bruno smiled ear to ear. "Si, as do I for you. You are a good young man Serafin. In fact, I think of you like a son. So, get to the point. You and I are not ones to speak in oration."

Serafin hesitated. "Um.. well, you know that I have been working hard."

"Si" Bruno smiled.

"And, I have saved quite a bit of money."

Bruno nodded while lighting his DeNobili.

"And... Well..." Serafin couldn't believe how nervous he was.

"Proseguire..." Bruno filled an extra glass with wine and offered it to Serafin.

Serafin took the wine and nervously sipped it. Finally, Serafin mustered up the spirit to speak.

"Well, I was wondering if I could obtain permission to court your daughter, Petrina. I will respect her and I will provide for her and put a roof over her head like you taught me!" Serafin blurted it out like a rapid fire gun. He spoke so quickly that even he had trouble keeping up. He stopped and looked at Bruno nervously.

Bruno paused, took a puff on his cigar, and then broke out in a roaring laugh, he had been expecting this, actually, not that he would ever let on, hoping for this moment.

"Serafin! Calmare!" He placed his hand on Serafin's shoulder. "Mio figlio. I thought you would never ask! Of course you have my permission. What do you think you have been doing?"

Serafin smiled nervously and sunk into his chair slightly. Bruno continued. "You two are practically a couple now. Everyone in the city knows the two of you as good, respectful people! I couldn't be happier. You know that I am getting older and it is important for a father to find a good husband for his daughters. I am pleased, very pleased."

Serafin was taken aback. "But, I am not Italiano. Do not you want.."

Bruno cut him off. "Serafin, none of us are perfetto." Bruno laughed deep and hearty. "But... Cornuto… You will do… I guess!"

With that Bruno and Serafin stood up and Bruno embraced Serafin.

Just as suddenly, Bruno ceased the frivolity and turned serious once again. "Now, go. You have your work ahead of you. She may not like you!"

Bruno continued laughing to himself as he resumed his place in his chair amongst his grape vines.

Edward J. Indovina

Chapter 20

Behold! I tell you a mystery. We shall not all sleep, but we shall all be changed.
1 Corinthians 15:51

Remy was silent during dinner. The kids and Rachiel noticed it and tried not to pry. After dinner the kids retired to their rooms and Rachiel cleaned up after them. Remy remained seated at the table and just stared blankly ahead of himself. Finally, Rachiel took a seat at the table across from Remy and broke the silence.

"Rem, what's up? Anything I can do?"

He let out an extended sigh. "No Rach. No. Thank you though."

"Well, what's up? What's wrong?"

"Rach, I don't know what to do anymore. Today I went to Social Services and what a freakin' joke. Did you know that we can't get help unless we cheat the system?"

Rachiel smiled easily. "Um... No, I didn't."

Remy leaned back in the chair and looked up at the ceiling. "I just can't do this anymore. Nothing's coming, nothing's happening. I'm useless!"

Rachiel slapped the top of the table with palm of her hand. "Ramiel Serafin Gayo! I will not have you call yourself useless! And what about the speech you gave me the other day? Did that suddenly evaporate?"

Remy looked at his wife with an exasperated look of defeat. "I just can't do it anymore, Rach. I just can't do it. I'm ready to give up."

"Give up? Why?" Rachiel was starting to lose her composure now. Defeatist talk was very low on her level of toleration.

"I just said, NOTHING's happening. Everything I do is just more failure." Remy's arms went up in dramatic fashion waving the air.

"Well, Ok, so things are tough right now. But that's no reason to give up!"

"Why NOT?" Remy's voice was starting to rise. "What ELSE have I got? What the fuck is the difference if I give up! In fact, why don't I just end it all and let you and the kids live off the insurance MONEY! I'M A FAILURE! ALL THE LOW LIFES HAVE IT MADE, WHAT DO I HAVE!!"

Remy was shaking and his voice shrill. Rachiel, instead of receding grew more angry herself. She stood up from her chair and started pointing her finger at Remy. "HOW DARE YOU!" Remy raised his head quickly at his wife's retort.

"You selfish, egotistical, spoiled, lazy bastard! How dare you think of taking the coward's way out! I'll kill you before I let that happen!" Rachiel tried to suppress her smile when she realized what she had just said, but her anger kept her demeanor as she continued.

"What makes you think that you have it so bad? Why? Because you can't just up and find a job in a day? Look at you. I think that you've forgotten how good you have it still. You get unemployment, you still have our savings, I'm trying to help and yet you have the nerve to sit there and mope instead of doing anything about it!"

Remy started to speak but Rachiel jabbed her finger in the air at him. "Don't. I'm not finished yet. Do you think that I don't miss some of the luxuries we had? Do you think that I don't miss working less hours? Yes, I do. But I know that it's necessary right now to help save OUR family. Remember? YOU AND I!" she rolled on. She took a deep breath and lowered her voice.

"So, let me tell you something, mister. My father didn't have those safety nets when he came over and neither did your father or grandfather. They had nothing! Nothing but their will and their drive. They didn't have unemployment insurance, welfare, or any of those things. Instead, what they had was the courage and will to make something out of their lives. Maybe that's the problem. Maybe you need to have everything taken away from you to see if you have the drive. I wonder if you do!"

Remy stared at his wife blankly. He couldn't believe what he had just heard. Of course, Rachiel herself was taken aback slightly at her outburst. This had obviously been building up in her.

Remy looked at his wife sheepishly and opened his mouth to speak but nothing came out. Finally, after what felt like an eternity he was able to speak.

"Rach, I...I don't know what to say. I..I guess you're right"

Rachiel sat down exhausted and cradled her head in her hands. Now that the adrenaline had worn off she felt awful about the way she had just spoken to her husband. "I'm sorry honey, I know you're frustrated but you've got to pick yourself up. You also have to realize, this isn't just about you, and we're all hurting from this. Me and the kids, it kills us to see you this way."

Remy swallowed hard and stared at her. She was right, her words hit hard. He started to think about her words and replay them over in his head. Remy took a deep breath, finally lifted his head and looked at his wife.

"No, you're right Rach. I have been a whiner. I keep comparing myself to people I shouldn't compare myself to. I mean, I lived..., I live a good life. Just because the sciviats want to live like they do doesn't mean that I should join or be envious of them. Let them have their food stamps, section eight, and welfare. That's no way to live, I don't want it."

A smile came over Rachiel's face. "Well...um, I'm glad to hear it I guess."

"And another thing" Remy continued. "You mentioned my grandpa and our dads. You're right. They had it a lot harder than we did and look what they accomplished."

Rachiel smiled wearily at her husband. "Well, remember what my dad used to say, "Stop talking and start doing."

Remy smiled, "Or what my grandpa said, "Nothing is accomplished by commiserating about it."

Remy looked at his wife quietly now. "I can't believe how much I love her," he thought to himself. It's human nature to begin to ignore what is constantly in front of us or what we already have. What we once found stunning and coveted becomes, literally, a part of the immediate scenery once it has been acquired. It takes a change in perspective, or jolt to the system to help us realize what it was in the first place that made us pursue it as much as we did. Remy had just had that jolt as he re-realized the beauty and wonderment of his wife, Rachiel.

Remy moved over to his wife and grabbed her in his arms and hugged her hard. "God, I love you."

"I love you too, Rem."

"Rach, I never heard you like that."

"Well, I never heard you like that. I'm so sorry I yelled at you."

Remy smiled, "I deserved it." Remy pulled back and looked into her eyes.

"Oh, by the way. You're going to kill me if I kill myself?"

Rachiel smiled sheepishly. "Well, you made me mad with that talk!"

They but broke down laughing, hard. "Well, I'll be damned if anyone is going to kill you but me, you big jerk!"

"I'll have to keep that in mind."

Rachiel pulled back and leaned against the kitchen counter, grabbed a bottle of wine from the refrigerator and took two glasses down from the cupboard. Remy took a seat at the kitchen island. Rachiel joined him with the two glasses of wine and placed Remy's in front of him.

"So, husband of mine, what's next?"

Remy looked across the island at his wife with a smile, "Yes, what is next? I think I have an idea?"

Chapter 21

The courtship of Serafin and Petrina wasn't as much a courtship as a culmination of sorts. As far as the community, or the neighborhood, at large was concerned, they were already a couple.

The merchants looked forward to seeing the handsome couple as they did the shopping for Bruno's family every week and actually were disappointed when they didn't show up.

Serafin knew, however, that he needed to get some things in place before he could ask Petrina's hand in marriage. It was a large responsibility to take care of a wife and he wanted to make sure that he was prepared. He marked off the list in his head, he needed a job, savings, and a place to live. The job he had, the savings he had, the only thing left was a place to live. He wanted to show Bruno and Regina that he was a good provider for their daughter and that they did not make a mistake by allowing him to court Petrina.

The next morning Serafin arrived at work. Before he could even get his coat off in the locker room, Salvatore came in to give Serafin a message.

"Cornuto, Giuseppe would like you to see him in his office!"

Serafin looked at Salvatore slightly surprised. "Cio che?"

"Non so, Cornuto. He just told me to get you when you came in."

Serafin nodded quietly and walked up the hall towards Giuseppe's office. His mind started racing. What did he do? He had been to work on time every day and he hadn't taken a day off since starting here. Even on days when he wasn't feeling strong he still came in and did the best that he could. Although he knew that negative thoughts lead to negative occurrences he couldn't help but be slightly nervous.

Serafin approached the open door of Giuseppe's office. He took a deep breath and entered.

As Serafin walked in Giuseppe motioned with his hand for Serafin to take a seat. Giuseppe was standing at the credenza preparing himself a cup of coffee. Serafin sat in the hard wooden chair in front of Giuseppe's desk. Giuseppe himself took a seat at his desk and smiled over at Serafin.

"Serafin, Buongiorno. Or should I say, Buenos Dias?"

"Buongiorno Giuseppe." Serafin responded slightly nervous. His mind raced again, was he working hard enough? Did he upset someone? Serafin fought to contain his emotions as he sat pensively.

"Serafin, relax. I can tell that you are nervous. There is nothing to be nervoso."

Serafin visibly attempted to relax in his chair but to no avail, his mind raced nervously.

Giuseppe smiled broadly. "Quindo, capisco che si vuole sposare la figlia di Bruno, Petrina?"

Serafin smiled broadly at the name of Petrina. "Si, how do you know?"

Giuseppe laughed broadly and deep. "There is very little that I do not know, Cornuto! You will discover that fact!"

Serafin smiled. Suddenly all of the anxiety and fear washed away from his body. Now he truly settled into the chair with a calm repose. "I am courting Petrina, Si."

"Bene, bene! She is a fine young girl, and you, you are a good young man!"

Serafin smiled embarrassedly. In the pits he never heard any feedback on his performance. In fact, no one ever really communicated or bothered with him as long as he was working. To hear this bit of praise felt good to Serafin.

Giuseppe leaned back in his chair and took a sip of his coffee. "Serafin, you have been doing well for us here. I respect you for your work and your dedication. But, more than that, I respect you as a man. You have proven yourself with your efforts and results."

Serafin answered nervously and humbly. "Gracias, Giuseppe. Sei troppo gentile."

"Nonsense. You have earned all of your praise, now, I must speak to you about another matter."

Serafin leaned forward in his chair towards Giuseppe, who continued. "If I may be so bold, I have an offer for you."

Serafin cocked his head at this.

"I have a home, on First Street, not far from here. I was renting it to another couple and they moved on. Now, I would like to offer it to you. You can pay me every month and the amount that you pay me would go to the purchase of the home or just towards rent and you can save for a home on your own."

Serafin was flabbergasted. He could not believe the kindness offered by Giuseppe. He became so nervous he started sweating.

" Yo, no se` que`decir..."

Giuseppe laughed out loud. "Serafin, I am good at translating, but even that.."

Serafin caught himself, he always reverted to his native tongue when he became nervous or angry.   "Scusi, Giuseppe. I don't know what to say."

"What you can say is that you will do it! Bruno has become a good friend of mine, and I consider his children to be e nipote. Therefore, the last thing I want is his precious daughter to marry a vagabondo!"

Giuseppe roared and leaned back in his chair. Serafin started to chuckle lightly in unison.

"Now, I will take you to the home during our lunch break. Oh, and one more thing. The home has an upstairs apartment that I am having mia Madre stay in. Just promise me that you will look in on her every now and then. Of course, knowing her, she will look in on you more often."

"Si, certo." Serafin rose from his chair and grabbed Giuseppe's hand while he was still seated and shook it anxiously.

"I will not let you down. I cannot believe the kindness that everyone has offered me in this country. Now, I must get to work so that I don't disappoint you on that front."

Serafin turned to exit the room Giuseppe motioned for him to pause.

"Serafin, you have earned every kindness that you have been given. Never, for one moment, should you think otherwise. You work hard, you are respectful, and you care about your work and your fellow man. That is all that anyone can ask. Remember, the Lord blesses a worker. It may not seem so at times but he does. The only thing that I ask is that you don't change and you help others when you are in the position to. That is all."

Serafin nodded knowingly and walked out to his job. "This is truly a great country" he thought as he exited.

Edward J. Indovina

Edward J. Indovina

Chapter 22

"Have a good day!" Remy announced to the kids. For the first time in a long time he had the old lift in his voice. However, the kids had heard this before the past few weeks and were hoping for a longer lasting moment this time.

"My, is that my Old Remy I see?" Rachiel teased.

"I don't know what you're talking about my dear! Now, don't you have something to do today?"

Rachiel playfully slapped him on the arm. "Now see here. What is it to you?"

"I've got work to do and maybe I don't want to be disturbed!"

Rachiel shook her head. "Ok, my master!" and she nodded her head in her best "I Dream of Jeannie" pose.

Remy poured himself a cup of coffee and proceeded to the den, then logged on to his computer and started setting his plan in motion.

First he contacted the Local election board via e-mail. He then began scanning all of the social network sites, taking notes of the hot topics and current conversations. As he poured himself into the research the time flew by. In fact, he was startled when he heard the kids come home from school.

"Hey dad." the voice carried over from the foyer as Sari took off his shoes and threw his book bag onto the floor.

Remy came out of the den and greeted his son. "Oh, Hello Sari. How was school today?"

Sari finished hanging up his jacket and turned to his father. "Good, good. How 'bout you? What did you do today dad?"

Remy smiled and tussled his son's hair. "Tell you what, let's grab a snack from the kitchen and you can tell me about your day."

Sari looked at his father hoping to hear more. "Sure dad, but, did it go okay today?"

"Great Sari, great. I'll let you all in on it during dinner tonight" Remy opened the refrigerator and threw an apple at Sari.

"Okay dad."

Sari was intrigued. He hadn't heard this type of excitement in his father's voice in a long time. Actually, he thought that this time it sounded legitimate. He actually couldn't wait until dinner.

Six-thirty arrived and everyone was seated at the dining room table. When Rachiel had entered the door Sari had whispered to her his father's excitement. As she served dinner all eyes were on Remy and he knew it.

Remy felt their anticipation and decided to play with everyone.

"So, I guess you're all wondering why I asked you here tonight." Sari and Angela started giggling.

"Actually dad, if you didn't have food I was going to be too busy to attend!" Angela said between chews of her food.

Everyone broke out laughing.

Remy filled his dish with spaghetti and sauce he made a grand gesture with his hands. "Well, there, I have food. Now, do you want to hear my news?"

Rachiel feigned boredom and rolled her eyes. "Oh, I guess so, don't you just so want to know kids?" she deadpanned.

Remy smiled from ear to ear. "Well, Ok. Remember how I used to tell you guys that if you don't like the way things are, that instead of griping about it you should work to change it?"

The kids looked at one another and nodded their heads in unison.

"Umm.. Yeah." Sari and Angela responded in chorus, Rachiel just looked on expectantly waiting to hear what was coming next.

Remy continued. "Well, after doing some extensive research I found out that there are an awful lot of people who feel the way I do. People who are dissatisfied with the way things are turning out to be in this country."

Sari was the first to ask. "Like what dad? The way what things are turning out?"

Remy addressed his son. "Well, Sari, you may be a little young yet, but there was a time when we all didn't have to struggle just to get a job and support our families. It used to be that if you worked hard and did the right thing that you could earn your way in life. Now, regardless of what I and your mother try to do for you, I'm beginning to worry about what you kids will have to go through."

"Okay, so what does this mean?" Rachiel pressed.

Remy was still evasive, "Well, what it means is that we need to be a voice in this country once again."

Rachiel replied to Remy "Rem, who is we?"

Remy answered indignantly. "We, the middle class! The workers! The ones who are always forgotten about but are the backbone of this country!"

"Rem, things haven't always been easier. It's always been a struggle."

Remy looked strongly at his wife. "Rach, I'm not saying it hasn't, but, It certainly hasn't been like this. In this environment it feels as though everyone is just out to keep squeezing you."

Rachiel was beginning to think the worse now. What crazy thing was he planning? "Remy, our parents went through hard times too. Are you sure you aren't feeling this way because of what you're going through?" She was starting to get worried that Remy was contemplating doing something stupid.

Remy smiled as he took a bite of his food. "Rach, I know what you're thinking. And, it's yes and no because of what I've been going through. I've been spending a lot of time commiserating about what happened instead of looking for a solution to it. Instead of looking for people and things to blame for my lot in life I should have been working towards correcting it."

Remy took another bite of his food and continued. In the meantime everyone was quiet around the table and waiting for the next words. "You know, I've been doing a lot of thinking about my situation. And there is a lot of blame that I can look upon myself. I didn't prepare myself well and I should have worked harder at improving myself like getting a degree from college." He stared at his children as he finished that statement.

"Dad, you know I'm…" Sari started to say until Rachiel shushed him.

"The other thing that this situation has done is make me think about my father and how he approached tough times. You know, I never remember my father whining about misfortune. He always seemed to carry himself with a quiet grace. I used to watch him encounter disappointment and he would just appear to shrug it off."

Remy started to choke up like he usually did when he talked about his father. He took a deep breath and regained his composure.

"You know, I remember when my dad told me when he actually crossed a picket line to get to work. Everyone was screaming and yelling at him and threatening him with harm. I asked him why he did it if people were threatening to hurt him. He looked at me and said that if he didn't cross that line he wouldn't have been able to feed his family, and his family was the most important thing in the world to him."

Sari hung on these words. "Wow, Grandpa did that?"

Remy smiled. "Actually, Grandpa did more than just that. Once, during the race riots that took place in the city in the 1960s, your grandfather was headed to work. When he pulled up in his truck he saw that they were protesting and blocking the street on an early morning in July. Rocks and bottles were being thrown at all passing cars and trucks. No one could get through. Not even the police. Grandpa said that when they saw him pull up in his green delivery truck a bunch of them started waving to the others to let him through. A bunch of the rioters parted and let grandpa through with his truck."

Sari and Angela said in unison. "Wow."

Rachiel looked at Remy with curious intent. "Rem, even I didn't know that story" Rachiel continued looking at Remy with rapt attention.

"Well, Dad never really spoke about it. He just said that they let him through to get to work. Some of them said as he was driving through that 'he was one of the good ones.' My Dad used to hire some of the neighborhood kids to help him during his work day many times."

Remy paused and stared into space. "You know, I never really thought about it, but my dad, your grandpa, was always good to everyone. As long as they had an honest work ethic, my dad didn't care what they looked like, or their ethnicity." Remy paused again in thought.

Sari broke the pause. "Wasn't Grandpa scared?"

Remy laughed. "Yeah, yeah he was. He later told me that he was when I asked him the same thing. You know, until then I thought that nothing ever scared my dad. I always thought that he was the toughest man on the planet. Yet, that was the last time he ever brought that up. Even when he got sick with cancer he never brought it up again. And boy, did he tell stories when he got ill..."

Angela decided to ask the pointed question. "But, Dad. So, what's going on? I'm sure that it's more than telling stories about Grandpa."

Remy shook his head as if he were bringing himself in for a landing. "No, actually guys. I worked all day and will work for the next bunch of weeks. Family of mine, you're looking at this town's new candidate for State Senate!"

Rachiel looked at him in disbelief. "Rem, really?'

"Yep. I called the election board this morning. Got all the information e-mailed to me. Did my research on my campaign and tomorrow, I file the papers, collect the signatures and enter the race!"

They all sat there happy, but curious to this turn of events.

"Really? You're going to go through with this?" Rachiel asked.

Remy looked directly into his wife's eyes and answered emphatically. "Yes, Yes I am."

"But, but what made you decide to do this?"

Remy smiled and looked once again into his wife's eyes. "Rach, it's been way too long since the people have had a say in this government. We complain about it yet we have done nothing about it. And you know what's ironic? We, the middle class, allowed it to get this way through our apathy and indifference. That alone is amazing. Did you realize that as a whole, we, the middle class, are the biggest lobby in the country if we want to be?"

Rachiel looked at him. "A Lobby?"

"Yep, Rach, a Lobby; a group of citizens with a common agenda that petitions the government for its cause."

Rachiel smirked at Remy's use of a definition and twisted her face into a goofy look and uttered, 'duh.'

Remy smiled and ignored her. Rachiel straightened up and asked, "Do you really think that you'll make a difference?'

Remy continued. "Even if I don't make a difference directly, or lose, at least my message will get out there and stir things up. It will be like what used to happen in the original days of this country."

Rachiel started to think practical about this now. She was especially worried that Remy would waste the rest of their savings on this new found folly of his.

"But, what about the money to do this?" she asked.

Remy had anticipated this and smiled slightly at his wife.

"Well, I figured I'll start small. And, you know something? I've been moping around here and I figured what the heck. I'm better than that. I was brought up to know better. It's not like I'm running for Federal Congress, I'm running for a local race. I'm running for the 28th district!"

Sari started to ask. "But, Dad, how are you?..."

Remy finished Sari's thought. "I called up a few friends. John is building my website, Pete is hooking me up with printing fliers, Jack is going to help me with press releases, Cheryl is going to help me with my campaign copy."

Rachiel began to get excited for her husband. "Wow, sounds like you're serious about this."

Remy looked at all of them. "Damn right I am. It's not like I'm doing anything but spinning my wheels all day. This is it. I'm running and I'm going to win!"

"But what is your message going to be?" Rachiel asked, knowing full well what the answer was going to be.

"My message is: Enough is enough, of treating us, the middle class, like forgotten pariahs. We're the ones that fund everything in this country therefore we should have the most say of where that money goes. I'm running on a campaign of Social Services Reform, Tax Reform, and Job Creation."

Rachiel grinned, "Oh, boy, that's going to be eaten up by the press. Are you ready to be almost crucified?"

Remy looked seriously at Rachiel. "I thought about that. But, and here's the big but.. There appear to be so many people who feel my way that I don't think I have anything to lose. In the beginning, I'll take the heat but as we keep going the momentum of supporters should help me through."

Rachiel felt compelled and had to ask: "Who are these people who think like you? How do you know so? And, more importantly, do you think that they will support you?"

Remy answered self-assuredly. "I started to think about that very thing. Then I realized, we live in an information overload type of world now. Social media has exploded. If people aren't boring you with e-mails and texts they're airing their dirtiest and most boring laundry on Yourface , Moogle, and Qaucker. Therefore, I obtained an account with all of them and took notes on what people are talking about. I scoured all of the accounts and even the Bobslist 'Rants and Raves' board to get a feel for the attitude of the country. I then noted the most commonly discussed topics and have laid them out in this notebook."

He grabbed a spiral bound notebook from under his chair and displayed it to all of them.

Rachiel and the children answered almost in chorus.
"Well, I guess you really have thought this out."

Remy smiled broadly at this. Then they all started clapping. Remy looked a little stunned.

Rachiel was the first one to speak. "Honey, you know we're behind you through all of this. Whatever you decide." But, in reality, Rachiel wondered under her breath if he would actually carry this idea through this time.

With that, Remy's race for congress was on.

Chapter 23

He feels only the pain of his own body, and he mourns only for himself."
  Job 14:22

Serafin awoke in the morning with what had become the usual aches and pains. However, this time they felt worse than ever. When they first started he thought it was just old age and he ignored it. He continued to go to work at the Railroad and work as the foreman at the Trestle on Boxart Street. But, even though he didn't perform as much manual labor as before, it seemed that he became tired sooner and sooner as the days went on.

He washed up and made his way downstairs, then made his way to the kitchen where his wife Petrina and daughter Isabel were. The two women smiled and greeted him as he made seated himself.

"Good Morning Dad!" his daughter greeted him. Serafin smiled broadly at the sight of his youngest. She always brought a smile to his face no matter what was going on in his life.

Serafin and Petrina had built a good life together. After their marriage, Serafin had continued to pay the rent on the house he had rented from Giuseppe. After that home had been paid for Serafin and his wife realized that they would need more room for their growing family. While in the home on First Street, their first child was born. Josephine was a strong, healthy gift from God. Next, came another daughter, Phyllis. It was then that Serafin and his wife realized that they would need more room.

They took the earnings from the sale of the home on First Street and purchased their current home on Rohr Street. It was after they moved into their new home on that Isabel was born.

Petrina and Serafin were very proud of their children. They worked very hard together to raise their children. And, it wasn't easy.

Petrina stayed home and ensured that their home was a home to be proud of while her husband worked hard at the port. In the beginning, Petrina would travel daily to the market to purchase fresh food for the meals she would prepare during the day to make sure that when Serafin arrived home from work he would have a fine meal waiting.

As time continued, technology became more advanced. When they obtained a functioning refrigerator / freezer it was as if they had entered the space age. Now, Petrina could travel to the market only twice a week and feed her family. And, what she didn't have she could still purchase from the few remaining cart salesmen that sold produce and other such sundries.

"Dios!" Serafin exclaimed loudly before he hit the ground. As he attempted to sit down his feet went out from under him and he struck the tile floor in the kitchen hard.

"Dad!" Isabel rushed to her father's side and held him up. As he sat embarrassedly on the kitchen floor it was obvious to both his wife and daughter that not only had he lost his balance, he lost his senses momentarily.

"Come on, dad. Let's get you into your chair." Isabel grasped her father under his arms and helped to lift him. The boost gave Serafin enough strength to lift himself and as he grabbed the edge of the table he placed himself in the kitchen chair.

"Gr…Thank you." Serafin looked up at his daughter appreciatively. He caught himself talking his native tongue. He knew that his daughter wanted both he and his wife to speak English. In fact, it was the two of them that encouraged their children to speak only English. Serafin and Petrina realized that their children would have an easier route in this country if they spoke the native tongue of the land. In actuality, it was really an effort on his part to help his children avoid the struggle and prejudices that he experienced in his new country.

When Serafin first arrived in this country not only was he an immigrant in this country, he was literally an immigrant in the neighborhood he lived in. While Bruno and Regina welcomed him, many of the Italian immigrants did not due to his Spanish heritage. After he had decided to leave Bruno's home he encountered many a difficult time due to his ethnic background. It was after he watched the prejudices that he and his wife endured he decided that he wouldn't allow his children to go through what they did.

Isabel was the only child who still remained at home. The other two daughters had married fine men and moved on.

Isabel meanwhile, was being courted by a man whom Serafin considered a fine young gentleman. He was a hard worker and treated his daughter with respect.

In addition, while Petrina's daughters were like their mother, the one thing they weren't like, was the way they entered the work place. Of course, at this time in history, many women were not only welcomed, but encouraged to enter the work force. During World War II while many men were serving their country, a previously unprecedented number of women entered the work place. After the war, while many women were happy to resume their societal roles, others didn't mind remaining in the employment ranks.

Isabel knelt down eagerly next to her father. "Dad, we can't do this anymore! You're getting worse. We have to go back to the doctor!"

Serafin inhaled as deeply as he could. In fact, he couldn't even do that anymore. His breaths became shallower by the day. His daughter caught that and pressed her father with more insistence.

"Dad, I'm taking you to the doctor today!"

"No, no. That is not necessary. You have to go to work. It is merely an…ailment" as he said this he coughed, hard.

"Dad, enough. I will call in and I'll make up the time another day. You're more important!"

Serafin coughed again. "No, I am inconveniencing you. I will be fine."

Isabel glared at her father hard. The one thing you didn't want to do was to tell her no. In fact, if she was anything, it was like her father and when she had a task before her she was determined to see it through.

"Dad, I'm telling you now. Have something to eat and I will take you to the doctor. Understand?"

"Okay, Bien…"

Isabel sat next to her father and held his hand as she turned her head away from him. While at the same time Petrina stood by the sink and continued to wash the same dish over and over as she tried to hide her tears.

Chapter 24

The hand of the diligent will rule, while the slothful will be put to forced labor.
Proverbs 12:24

In the ensuing days Remy worked as hard as he had ever worked before in his life. While he considered himself as a 'grass roots' campaign it grew larger as his message got out. He discovered that as basic as his research was, it was accurate; there were a lot of people that felt the same way that he did. However, as usual, with all of the good came the bad.

Just like Rachiel had said, the local press went after him with sharpened tridents. "Racist runner," "Disillusioned Wanna Be Pol throws hat in ring," were among some of the kinder headlines bandied towards him. But, to his credit, Remy soldiered on, because his supporters were starting to trump the negative headlines and, almost in defiance, he actually started to gain national press coverage.

Many who believed in his message began to start sending in donations for his run, and some of them actually linked Remy's website on their own. Additionally, Remy's Meetbook page exploded with people joining his cause. The campaign and its message was bigger than he had ever realized.

Then, an attack hit home. When Rachiel was out doing the grocery shopping she was approached by two slick 'trap' reporters who cornered her as she was coming out of the store. As she exited the front doors of the supermarket a cameraman and young reporter approached Rachiel.

The young female reporter thrust a microphone in the face of Rachiel. "Excuse me, Mrs. Gayo? May we have a few words with you?"

"Yes?" Rachiel answered instinctively as she stared at the intrusive camera lens in front of her face. Her grip tightened on the shopping cart as if she would have to use it as a shield against these intruders.

The reporter continued. "We're from Channel 10 and we'd like to ask you about your husband's campaign."

By now a crowd was starting to gather around Rachiel and the reporters. Rachiel answered pensively. "Well, You would have to ask him about that, I don't really..."

The reporter cut her off. "Are you telling us that you have no say in the home?"

Rachiel stumbled again as the crowd started to mill around. "No, I didn't say that, what I was saying was..."

The reporter cut her off again. "Ms. Gayo, just what are you saying? That you don't support your husband's views? How does he treat you? Is he antagonistic towards women?"

The reporters pressed on with their line of questioning, this was their tactic, to make the interviewee provide them with a sound bite that they could exploit to attract viewers.

Rachiel, while she was doing her best to ignore them, became angry at the implication of her husband being a woman-hater. She answered them abruptly. "He never, in fact, trust me. He treats myself, my daughter, and any other woman in his life with the utmost respect. Unlike you, he was brought up with good moral values!"

Some of the crowd started to cheer. The reporter, a young African-American woman deftly ignored the comment and decided to go for the throat as she was taught by her peers. "Mrs. Gayo, are you and your husband racist?"

Rachiel looked at the woman incredulously. "Excuse me?'

The reporter suppressed a smirk. In the meantime some in the crowd started chanting, "Gayo, Gayo!"

"Well, your husband is running on a social services reform campaign. Does that mean you don't want to help people?"

Rachiel smirked herself. She started pushing her shopping cart towards the cameraman making him back up while filming her. The reporter started to follow Rachiel and the crowd moved with them.

Rachiel answered indignantly. "We never said such a thing"

"We? So you do support him?"

Rachiel approached her van. "Yes, yes I do. In fact, I think by the size of the crowd following us, so do many people."

Rachiel stopped at the rear of her van and took her hands off of the shopping cart. She pointed her finger at the reporter sternly. "And, shame on you for trying to lead me with those types of questions. If anyone is being mendacious towards women, it's you."

The reporter shrugged her head as if tossing her hair and continued her questioning tactics. "Then, are you against immigrants?"

Rachiel looked in total disbelief and shook her head as she grabbed the handle of the rear door of her van to open it. "Wait a minute. This line of questioning is over." Rachiel lifted the tailgate of her van quickly causing the cameraman and reporter to jump backwards to avoid getting struck by the door.

The reporter tried one last attempt to trip up Rachiel. "Mrs. Gayo, should we prevent all immigrants from coming over here?"

Rachiel put down a grocery bag in the back compartment of her van, tried to catch herself, and just lost it. "Look, for your information, we're all immigrants. In fact, genius, I'm sure if you do some research you'll discover that you are a descendent of immigrants. Therefore, why would we condone that type of behavior against them? And, you know what else? This line of ridiculous questioning is over for the moment! Good Day, people!"

Rachiel smiled wickedly at the reporter and then addressed the gathered crowd. "And, Thank you one and all who support my husband's campaign. We WILL have a voice once again!" As she said this she brought up her fist in the air.

The crowd broke out in a cheer and began to start heckling the reporters. With that, the reporters started to pack up their equipment and retreat for the safety of their van. Rachiel hurriedly loaded the balance of her groceries into the car and drove off, watching her rear view mirror for anyone else.

Edward J. Indovina

Chapter 25

"Dad, we're here."

Isabel steered the car into the parking lot as she parked the car in the front of the house she looked over at her father. "He looks so frail, Lord help him." she thought to herself. She exited the car from her door and rushed over to the passenger door to let her father out.

"Come on, Dad." as she opened the door her father sat still in the seat and looked up at the face of his daughter.

"Okay, just give me un minuto."

Isabel stood and watched as her father attempted to get out of the car. As Serafin swung his feet out Isabel grabbed his arm and essentially lifted her father out of the car. "My God, he almost weighs nothing now!" she thought to herself as she swung the car door closed with her hip as she walked him to the door of the doctor's office.

"Dad, let me help you!"

Isabel was beginning to get frustrated with her father. Every time she tried to support his weight he would pull away and try to walk by himself. As sick as he was, his pride carried him where his body wouldn't.

"Esperar"

"What? Dad, you know I don't…" Isabel knew what he meant even if she didn't want to admit it. She was making him nervous even though she was consciously trying not to.

"I'm sorry. Here, take my arm, Dad." She brought him to the door and opened it.

Isabel seated her father on a chair in the waiting room. After he was seated she approached the front desk in the room.

The waiting room was essentially the parlor of the house. The room was filled with chairs and two coffee tables covered with magazines. On the walls were mounted fish on ornate wooden plaques. Towards the rear of the room was a freshwater aquarium, apparently an attempt to provide calmness to the prospective patients.

The receptionist/doctor's wife smiled and addressed Isabel.

"Hello, do you have an appointment today?"

"No, no we don't. The name is Gayo, Serafin Gayo. He is a regular patient here. But, please, my father is getting worse. I know that the doctor said he can't see anything but there has to be something. He's in so much pain and…"

The receptionist cut her off as Isabel rambled on rapid fire.

"I understand. Let me get the doctor and we'll see what we can do." She stood up and walked into the rear examining room as Isabel leaned against the corner of the desk and looked in the direction of her father. Serafin slumped in the chair and his head leaned forward.

"My God, he looks so weak," Isabel thought to herself as she took a nervous deep breath.

"Miss?" The receptionist's voice broke her out of thoughts and she looked up

"Yes?"

"You and your father follow me to the side examining room."

Isabel went over to her father and urged him to rise and follow her. Serafin looked up at his daughter with a smile and attempted to stand up. Seeing that her father was having difficulty she grasped his arm and helped him up. Serafin used his daughter's arm to help walk to the room.

Serafin sat gingerly in the examination room chair. In addition to the examination table was a large, shrouded machine. Isabel tried to examine it, but it was covered with a white sheet. Before she could lift the sheet the doctor arrived in the room.

"Ah, Serafin. I understand you still aren't feeling well."

"Doctor. Please, I know you haven't been able to find anything, but he seems to be getting worse. I mean, look at the weight he's lost!"

The Doctor studied Serafin with his eyes. While his speech didn't reflect it, his facial expressions betrayed his true feelings. He was worried. His patient didn't look good and it was weighing on him. This was a man who was only in his fifties for God's sake. What was it he was missing?

"Let's see what we can do." He muttered as he reviewed the past chart of Serafin. There was no doubt about it, while his age was listed as fifty-seven he appeared presently to be in his late sixties.

Finally, the Doctor broke the silence. "Umm, I want to try something. Now, normally I wouldn't use this type of machine but we have to get somewhere."

Isabel nodded in agreement. "Anything, Doctor. I can't stand to see him like this."

Doctor Williams smiled; he reached over and pulled the sheet off of the machine. "This is a full body fluoroscope. Now, the State has asked us to refrain from using these machines because reports have shown that they can cause radiation cancer. However, to be honest with you, there is no better machine to show if your father has what I suspect."

"Fluoroscope. Isn't that what they use to measure feet?"

"Yes, yes it is. Only this one allows us to see various parts of the body wherever we position the screen. A fluoroscope will show us soft tissues as well as hard tissues."

Isabel didn't care anymore whether the machine sang or danced. All she cared about was would the machine tell them what was wrong with her Father.

"Okay, what do we do Doctor?"

Doctor Williams began putting on his lead lined gloves "Get your father over here and position him in between the screens here." He pointed with a now gloved finger.

Isabel walked over to Serafin who had already begun to get up, albeit with great difficulty.

"Dad! Hang on, you are so stubborn!" Serafin smiled weakly

"Estoy bien! Vamos a terminar con esto!"

"Sure Dad. Whatever you say!" Isabel helped her father walk towards the machine.

"Doctor, should he take off his shirt?"

"No, he'll be okay with it on." Isabel helped to position her father behind the screen.

"All right, Isabel, step back behind me please. We don't need you to be irradiated also!"

Doctor Williams placed the red goggles over his eyes and turned on the machine. The bright glow of the x-ray tubes projected their image through Serafin onto the fluorescent plate in the front of his body. The screen displayed what the doctor had suspected.

Dr. Williams turned off the machine and rocked his head forward. He grabbed his goggles and removed them while keeping his head down. As his right hand reached up and grabbed his forehead he finally spoke. "Serafin, thank you, go sit down in the waiting room. I'll talk to you and your daughter in a bit."

Isabel helped her father out of the room and looked over at the doctor as he continued to sit in front of the fluoroscope.

Chapter 26

Rachiel pulled into the driveway visibly shaken. She was so unnerved by the reporters' ambush that she didn't bother to grab the groceries and just ran into the house. Remy heard her come in and came out of the den.

Remy took one look at his wife's face and started to get nervous. "Rach, what's wrong?"

Rachiel, while she was the pillar of strength out in the crowd, now that she was in her sanctuary, started to break down. She ran to her husband as Remy went to go grab his wife but she paused.

"Remy, they got to me" she exclaimed as she fell into his arms.

Remy looked at his wife in terror. "Who babe? Who?"

Rachiel looked up at her husband with tears in her eyes. "The reporters! They were waiting for me at the grocery store!"

Remy shook his head. He was hoping this wouldn't happen but he also knew that it was inevitable and only a matter of time. "Rach, I'm so sorry. But, you yourself warned me about this type of thing happening, remember?"

"Yes, yes, I know" She was starting to calm down in his arms. "But, I didn't expect it! Least of all, to me!"

They moved over towards the couch and sat down. She didn't let go of Remy's hands. Remy put his arms around his wife and began to smile. Rachiel sensed his happiness and looked at him incredulously. She couldn't believe that he was getting pleasure out of this.

"Rach, do you know this means? Can I tell you something?" he said excitedly.

Rachiel looked up in her husband's eyes. "What? That you're a jerk who likes to watch his wife in agony?"

Remy smiled broader, and as much as he tried, he couldn't suppress it. "Honey, this is good news! It means the message, our message, is working!"

Rachiel pulled back and looked at him as though he were a madman. "What? Are you kidding?"

"Rach, it's true. They would have ignored you if they didn't think that we were going to do some damage. It's working! We're getting to them! They're scared!"

143

Rachiel looked at her husband incredulously at first, and then she looked at him with recognition that perhaps he was right.

"Do you really think so?"

"Absolutely"

Rachiel smiled and relaxed a bit. Although she wouldn't admit it, she was beginning to enjoy this if it was in fact true that they were causing the status quo pain. "Well, I hope I look good on TV. That bitch was lucky I didn't haul off and slap her, the indigenous idiot!"

Remy squeezed his wife's arm. "Whoa, Rach. She was just doing her job."

"Well, thank God I don't have to do that job. To stand there and act all high-and-mighty and ask such lying questions. Let me tell you something..."

Remy cut her off. "You are, you are. Come on, we're better than that. She's just a tool who'll get hers one day."

"Yeah, I guess you're right. Of course, it couldn't be soon enough in my book." She took a deep breath. "Anyways, yeah, let's see how I look on TV."

Remy smiled and gave his wife a big hug. "You're right. Order a Pizza and let's see." Remy put his arm around his wife and his mind wandered back to their beginnings.

Chapter 27

The righteous man perishes, and no one lays it to heart; devout men are taken away, while no one understands. For the righteous man is taken away from calamity.
Isaiah 57:1

The days seemed to pass as months to Serafin's youngest child. It was so difficult to comprehend. Her father, the strongest man she knew, reduced to lying in bed like this. She looked down at her father's frail body on the bed and shook her head. Yet, she knew one thing, she couldn't show weakness. No, that isn't what her father would do. What did he always tell her? "Weakness is the devil's tool. It is an instrument that he uses which causes you to embrace hopelessness. That, in turn, has you abandon one of the great gifts God gives us, which is hope. Because, the devil knows, that when man has hope, he fears nothing, which means you will not fear him."

Isabel was thinking all of this when she grasped her father's hand. "Dad, do you need anything?" at the sound of his youngest child's voice, his eyes opened.

"Eh, no, no…" he smiled up at her. "You, you look so much like your mother." His eyes closed and he fell back asleep.

Isabel walked out of the room. It was becoming hard to bear now. The deterioration of her father to the ravages of cancer was crushing her. What an evil, merciless disease she thought. To take a man who once was able to shovel an entire hopper of coal, come home, tend to the garden and then to the house, and render him bedridden was unthinkable. Although it was six weeks ago, it felt as if it was only yesterday that Dr. Williams had come out into the waiting room with the news. The cancer had moved throughout his whole body, the doctor said. The scope showed that it had traveled into his bones, and there was no hope.

As she stood there transfixed, her concentration was broken. When she felt the hand on her shoulder she jumped slightly. Startled she turned quickly and saw her mother's face. "Oh, mom…" that was it. She started sobbing uncontrollably at the sight of the only soul she would have left to turn to. As she fell into her mother's arms a year's worth of grief poured out of her.

145

"Ci là, tesoro. va tutto bene."

"Huh, what, mom?" Isabel regained some of her composure. It was ironic in a way. Both of her parents spoke in their native tongues when they encountered stress. And, being a child of America, of course, Isabel didn't understand a word of it.

"I'm sorry. I really am. I just can't stand to see daddy like this."

Before her mother could answer, their thoughts were interrupted by the voice of her husband, Isabel's father.

"Please, no te deseperes." He coughed violently, and raised his head. However, before he could say anything further, the moment was interrupted by more voices. As mother and daughter turned their heads to the direction of the voices Serafin smiled broadly and laid back with his head on the pillow.

"Hello, Mom?"

"Hello?"

The voices stopped as they entered the bedroom.

"Oh, there you are." The oldest daughter, Josephine said as she walked into the room. Her eyes went immediately to her father lying in bed and she rushed to the bedside.

"Dad, how do you feel?" she exasperated as she sat on the edge of the bed.

"Eh, Multa." he smiled broadly at his oldest daughter.

"Yeah, doesn't he look fine, Jo? Nice of you to visit."

"You know something, Bell? "

"No, what Jo?" Isabel paused a second. "You're right, sorry. At least you made it into the room, right Phil?" her eyes looked towards the doorway.

"Um, look. I'm trying!" Phyllis's eyes were frozen in the direction of her father. Yet, she couldn't find the courage to enter the room.

"Lay off, Bell! Enough. We're here now, isn't that enough?"

Isabel was about to answer in her patented cynically manner when out of the corner of her eye she saw her niece, Diana, standing in the doorway of the bedroom. She caught herself and tried to relax.

All of the emotions of anger and helplessness rose to the surface, yet she realized that it would do no one any good to carry on with them. Especially not her niece. No, not here. The worst thing a child should have to deal with is the loss of innocence that comes with the death of a loved one. On top of that, to witness fighting among family members would make it even worse. While it is an important passage in life, it still doesn't make it any easier to accept a child going through that. In the meantime the women turned and looked at their father.

"He looks so still, you don't suppose?" Josephine said aloud. But, before Isabel had to respond, the tension was broken by the family's patriarch.

"My girls, my beautiful girls are all here!" Serafin weakly lifted his head from his pillow and smiled.

"Dad!" the three voices cried out almost in unison. In the meantime, Petrina sat down in the chair next to the bed and simply stared at her husband with a distant look in her eyes. Serafin started laying his head back on the pillow when he suddenly came forward. "Grandpa?"

The sound of his granddaughter's voice sparked new life into his ailing body.

"Diana, little one." His smile radiated wide but he couldn't keep his head upright and he fell back onto the pillow.

Isabel grabbed her face with her right hand, clutched her mother's shoulder with her left and shook her head. "It's not fair, it's not fair."

"What? What isn't fair Bell?"

"This, all of this. He's not old enough to die! Not like this."

"Bell, it happens. This happens. What do you..."

"He's a good man! He's never done anything bad! Is this what you get for being good?"

Serafin broke the moment. "Para, para. Isabella, please." He paused. "You are so much like my mother, strong and opinionated. Do not worry yourself. I have no regrets, no ira. Look, look at what I have. My beautiful wife, the daughters she gave to me, and even grandchildren!. The Lord has determined to bless me. What else could a man want?"

Tears lined their faces now. No more words were needed to be said. As Serafin rested his head against his pillow once again Petrina started to recite the Lord's Prayer. Serafin's breathing grew more difficult now. As his left hand struggled underneath the sheet to come out. Phyllis reached out and lifted the sheet to free his hand. When he felt his hand free he reached out for his wife's hand. Petrina, without even looking reached out and grabbed her husband's hand.

Serafin smiled weakly and turned his head towards the love of his life. "Mia moglie, il mio amore, grazie. When I was a young man, here in the new world, I knew nothing, and no one. I was alone and nervous. Then, you and your family showed me kindness and it was then that I knew that I would make it. I would make something of myself in this land from God."

He coughed hard.

"Dios, Gracias dios. Thank you, thank you for a strong and beautiful family and for a beautiful life..."

His eyes closed as he took his last breath among the sobs and tears of the beloved women in his life.

Chapter 28

Meeting Rachiel was easy enough; they both had a mutual Social Studies class together in the community college. Of course, she sat in the front and Remy sat in the rear of the class never paying attention like he should. He treated Community college as though it was an extension of high school and as though it was his job to still be the class clown. Yet, in actuality, it was his sense of humor that first brought him to Rachiel's attention. Again, that was easy enough, but, it was meeting her parents that would be a hard sell if he was to court their daughter, especially if he was unemployed.

Remy's future in-laws arrived to America from Sicily during the 1940s. Rachiel's father, Salvatore, had had enough of Umberto Mussolini and his reign of oppression. In the beginning, Mussolini's policies seemed to help the country, but as time wore on, an overall feeling of oppression hung like a cloud over Italy as a whole and Salvatore thought it was time for a new start. They settled here in America and Salvatore went to work on the assembly line at the local manufacturer. It was a good life here in this new country, Salvatore thought. He was allowed to bring up his two children with a roof over their head and plenty of food to eat without the constant feeling that the government wanted to take their possessions and freedom away.

Here, in America, if you worked hard you could achieve much he often thought. Owning a home also wasn't a far away dream like it was in Italy. In fact, many people did, it was an essential part of the American Dream that was preached here. Homes were affordable, schools were good, and there was freedom to make your own choices. Granted, it wasn't easy being an Italian immigrant, but it was doable. In fact, that's why many neighborhoods began to be populated by people of similar ethnicities. The 'little' Italy's, 'little' Irelands, 'little' Polands and, even the Chinatowns, were evident in turn of the century America. While the neighborhoods still existed relatively untouched in the 1960s they had begun to become more integrated and less ethnic exclusive. Still, the old adage if you worked hard and respected others it would get easier never diminished. After all, the majority of the people in this country were immigrants of one sort or another.

When Remy first met Salvatore he knew that it would be a tough road to gain his favor. Remy had a few things going against him, not only was he an idealistic child, he wasn't even fully Italian. Salvatore looked at Remy with what Remy imagined as contempt at their first meeting. It wasn't until later that he realized that Salvatore was merely sizing him up. After all, who was this 'medican' to court his precious daughter? Like all Italian fathers, actually fathers of all backgrounds, no one was good enough for his daughter, particularly not a non-Italian boy with what appeared to be little to no prospects in life.

Remy pulled up in front of the house in his car. The car wasn't new but it also wasn't a piece of junk. Handed down to him from his parents the 1977 Mercury Comet had seen better days, but it was well maintained, The driver's door showed some signs of rust while the hood had a good sized dent in it from a shopping cart encounter. Remy got out of the car and stared across the lawn.

In front of him was a two story cape cod with two trees in the front yard and an attached garage. From the street view it had a pastel quality that was like looking at a Jessica Rohrer painting. The paved driveway led up to the screened doors that in the summer, replaced the standard garage door. As he walked up the drive he noticed that in addition to the screen doors, the garage had been converted into an open air family room. A couch, chair and refrigerator were in the makeshift family room along with the remnants of its winter purpose of a garage with work bench, shovels and hoses. Next to the refrigerator were wooden cases of beer and pop stacked 5 high.

As Remy walked down the paved concrete walk towards the front door he self-consciously swallowed hard and smoothed his hair before he knocked on the door. While he waited nervously he gave a quick look at his clothes. He was wearing chinos and a button up collared shirt. As he rubbed his chin he self-consciously thought that maybe he should have shaved again. "Well, it's too late now" he thought. Besides, Rachiel liked his scruffy look. She said it made him look "smart, in a professorial way". "You know" she teased, "like those older, smarter professors who go out with their students!" Remy loved it when she became playful. It made him feel at ease and comfortable like the world in which he was brought up in.

Remy took a deep breath and rapped on the door. He stood nervously waiting for a response. Suddenly, his wandering mind was abruptly interrupted as Michael; Rachiel's younger brother opened the door.

"Ratser! Your BOYFRIEND is here!!" he announced as though he was a Carnival Barker then, giggling, ran off. Michael was 10 years younger than Rachiel. At seven years old, he was lithe and trim and fast as a gazelle.

Remy entered the house by one step and froze in the doorway. He quickly looked around and saw that the foyer floor was a parquet floor while to his right was a mirror and below that, a shoe rack. To his left was a series of pegs where jackets were hung. While Remy was looking at his immediate surroundings his peripheral vision caught Salvatore rising from his recliner chair. All Remy saw was the back of Salvatore's head. As Salvatore rose from his chair he appeared to be ten feet tall to a tremulous Remy. The irony was that in reality Salvatore was a very normal Five foot six inches.

As Salvatore turned, Remy suddenly felt extremely discomfited. Remy felt as though Salvatore's eyes were peeling away layers of his once confident self. Salvatore looked Remy up and down quizzically as he approached Remy.

Salvatore broke the awkward silence between the two men. "So, You are-a Remy?" Salvatore broke the silence.

Remy swallowed hard. "Y-yes, sir"

Salvatore stopped approximately three feet in front of Remy. "Mmmm, hmm. And, what do you do?"

Remy tried nervously to disseminate the question in his head. "Excuse me?"

"What do you do, do you work or go to school?"

Remy suddenly became mute. As hard as he tried to answer nothing came out. Remy wished in vain for Rachiel to descend the stairs and save him. Alas, it was not to be, he would have to endure this line of questioning that much longer.

Remy gathered his wits and finally answered Salvatore. "Umm, well, right now, sir, I'm, um, in between college and a job."

Salvatore jocosely looked at the young man. "In between? What is that? Either you are, or you aren't." Salvatore paused effectively. "Well, what is it?"

Remy gulped hard. "Umm, sir, that is, College isn't really working out for me, so I figured I would take a break."

"A break? I don' unnerstan' You mean you don't go?"

Remy swallowed hard before he answered. "Ummm, yes sir. That's kind of it. I just need to figure things out."

Salvatore shook his head. "Well, if you don't figure it out, then maybe you get a job, right?"

Remy looked down from Salvatore's eyes. "Ummm... Yes sir. That is my intention."

Salvatore smiled without letting Remy see. "Remy, Intentions are one thing. Actions are another... remember that."

"Geez, sounds like my father." Remy thought to himself. He started praying hard for Rachiel to appear.

Salvatore broke the uneasy silence once again. "So, I unnastand that your name is Gayo, Correct?"

Remy looked up, adjusted his stature, and smiled. He was proud of his last name. "Yes sir."

"Eh, what is that?"

Remy didn't understand the question again. "Excuse me?"

Salvatore defined the question for his young guest as best as he could. "What region is that from? I mean, where are your parents from?"

Remy smiled and relaxed a bit. "Oh, my father is from over on Norton Street."

Salvatore smiled and lightly chuckled aloud. "No, I mean, where was your father born?"

"Oh. He was born here. In Rochester." Then it hit him. "Well, my grandpa came over here from Spain if that's what you mean, and my grandma and other grandparents are from Italy."

Salvatore smiled. "Oh, okay. I ask because the name Gayo sounds familiar. I knew a family by the name of Gayo in my native Italy."

"Really?" Remy started to ease up a bit.

"Si, so, where in Spain did your grandfather come from?"

Remy answered proudly. "From San Tome, Spain. He used to tell us stories all the time."

Salvatore nodded. "That's good. A young man should know the family history."

"Yessir, you're right. Grandpa Serafin said that also."

"Serafin? That was your Grandfather's name? Do you know what his name means?"

Remy took a deep breath and smiled assuredly. This question he knew. Even though his grandparents never told him, he had looked the fact up himself. In fact, he found out by chance at his religion class when he was younger.

"Yes, yes I know. My grandpa was named after the highest order of angels. In fact, the Seraphim were the angels that fought the Great War in heaven and sent the devil down to his fate."

Salvatore grinned brightly at Remy's knowledge. "So, you do know something about your past and some religion also. Bene, bene."

Salvatore continued. "So, you are a Spaniard? No?"

Remy smiled answering this part of his interrogation. "Um, well, actually I'm part Spanish and part Italian, my Grandma Petrina was Italian so I guess you could say that I'm Italian."

Salvatore laughed. "Actually, if you are not truly Italian then you are not Italian."

Remy's smile faded with this statement.

Salvatore smiled and added, "However, never be ashamed of your true heritage. Don't discredit a part of your heritage because you have a need to fit in. You are you, and your heritage is a part of who you are. Be proud of your mixed heritage! Capisce?"

Remy smiled. "Si. Capisce"

Salvatore smiled ear-to-ear. "So, the not-so-pure knows a little Italian, eh?"

Remy answered becoming nervous again. "Well, at least I'm Catholic. Right?"

Salvatore burst out laughing. "Yes, yes. That helps! Of course, it doesn't mean that I like you, Spaniard!"

Reprieve finally arrived for Remy. Into the room, she burst like an angel of deliverance for Remy. Rachiel stood about five foot six inches and lean in frame. Her dark hair was cut in a mid-length style which framed her oval face.

Her white button up blouse and straight legged Levis with her white Converse sneakers made her appear playful and desirable at the same time.

"Daddy! " Rachiel's voice broke through the air. The moment he heard his daughter's voice Salvatore visibly relaxed. Regardless what was said or implied, Rachiel was the jewel in Salvatore's heart that motivated and drove him.

Salvatore looked at his daughter. He realized that his little Rachiel was growing into a woman and that he would no longer be able to keep her sheltered and to himself. Unfortunately he realized that it wouldn't be long until she left the house. She was growing into a woman he was proud of, and, there was the paradox that every parent faced. While no one liked to see their children leave the nest, it was a testament to the child's upbringing that they felt confident and assured to begin their own lives.

"Rachiel. Do you really want to go out with this boy?"

Rachiel's body language indicated that she ruled this battle right now. "Daddy, it's our first date. Don't scare him off like you do to all the rest!"

Salvatore feigned a hurt look. "I'm a just looking out for you. You know, make sure that this boy was worthy of my daughter."

Rachiel grinned and gave her father a kiss on his forehead. "Daddy, you're going to make me an old maid!"

Salvatore grinned. "Good, that is good for you. No man is good enough for my daughter!"

Rachiel grabbed Remy's arm and led him towards the door.

Remy couldn't leave fast enough; he looked back towards Salvatore as he was led out the door. "Sir, I will have her home by 11."

"Eleven?"

"Daddy!!" Rachiel gave her father a cross look.

Salvatore stood in the door way and shook his finger at the couple as they walked towards Remy's car.

"Okay. Now, You. You will drive carefully and no funny business with my daughter!"

Rachiel sneered at her father.

Salvatore softened the tone in his voice. "Okay, just get her home safe and sound!"

"Yes sir." as Remy was answering Rachiel rushed them out the door.

"Goodbye Daddy!"

Remy opened the passenger door of his car for Rachiel and walked over to the driver door while waving at Salvatore.

Salvatore watched as Remy's car drove down the street until the tail lamps faded out in the distance. From that time forward, Salvatore grew to love Salvatore like a son and Remy loved Salvatore like a second father.

Chapter 29

Remy and Rachiel poured their usual late night glass of wine. Only, instead of sitting in the kitchen area they sat on the couch in the sitting room waiting for the news. They turned to Channel 10 and waited. It wasn't long before they weren't disappointed.

There it was, on the Eleven O'clock News. In fact, it had been used as a leader story in the earlier ads of the night. "Tonight at 11, Local School Board denounces Mayor's plan for standardized testing, plus, is political hopeful Gayo a proponent for Illegal Immigration? We'll give you this and all the news on 10 at 11!"

"Hey, Ma. Is that gonna show you?" Angela asked as she was lying prone on the carpeted floor in front of the flat screen television located in front of the couch.

Remy smiled as he looked over at Rachiel. "I suppose so. But you'll never know, you'll be in bed by then!"

"Aw, c'mon! Can't we stay up? Please?!?!" Sari and Angela pleaded together as though they rehearsed it.

Rachiel looked at her husband with entreaty in her eye. "Remy, some help here?"

Remy smiled ear to ear and squeezed his wife's shoulder with his outstretched arm around her. "Well, Rach, why not? After all it isn't every day they see their mom on TV."

Rachiel beseeched Remy one more time. "No, I mean, it's too late for them to be up."

"Rach...." Remy implored.

The kids looked at Rachiel with their big eyes. In actuality, Rachiel was petrified at the thought of her family seeing her on television. What if she looked stupid? What if she embarrassed herself and Remy?

Rachiel looked to her husband for help with silence once again. Remy, while his wife may seem to think he doesn't pay attention to her, instantly recognized his wife's cry for help.

"Rach, relax. Whatever happens, happens. I'm sure you're going to look beautiful and intelligent, like we all know you, on the TV. Regardless of what the reporter tried to do to you. Heck, I'm proud of you for standing up to them! C'mon! The game is afoot! We're getting under their skin!" he exclaimed.

The kids started clapping and sat up in anticipation of the broadcast. Rachiel looked at her family and acquiesced.

"All right. But so help you guys if you don't get up in the morning. If you're late, you're father will have hell to pay!" She shook her finger at the children and her fist at Remy.

Remy looked at her in mock indignation. "Me? Hey, I'm just the political hopeful here. I don't think it would look good if I show up on camera battered and bruised!"

Rachiel glared at Remy and reiterated her prior threat. "Just remember kids, if you don't get up your father will look to be the Mummy candidate with all the bandages he'll be wearing!"

Finally the Eleven O'clock News started. The headline was like the teaser. "Now, for our top stories." The news anchor announced. "The Mayor encounters another setback in his quest for standardized testing in the City School District. Opposition from the teacher's union appears to send this item back to the negotiating table. Also, the wife of congressman hopeful, Remy Gayo, provides some insight to her husband's campaign? We'll get to these stories and more."

The station cut to a commercial after showing a quick shot of Rachiel standing behind her van.

Sari yelled out; "Hey, there you are Mom!"

Rachiel winced as she saw herself. "Geez, the camera really does add 10 pounds," she thought to herself.

Remy was smiling ear-to-ear as the program came back to the news stories. Finally they aired the piece.

Actually, Remy was pretty pleased with the clip and Rachiel was relieved. The editor was kind and cut out most of the disparaging questions from the reporter. In fact, if Remy and Rachiel didn't know better, it was almost as though the station looked unfavorably upon their staff reporter's line of questioning and attitude.

"Mom, you looked great!" Sari excitedly said.

"Yeah, you really looked p... ticked at that reporter!" Angela announced.

The piece didn't come off as bad as they expected. In fact, Rachiel's comment of "we're all immigrants" became the sound bite and gained steam as a viral video.

While the press attempted to turn the phrase into a negative, Remy's supporters turned it into a positive campaign message. Remy looked at his wife. "Honey, you did great! You were decisive, honest, and strong! Thank you so much!"

Rachiel smiled and shook her head. "Rem, I looked awful!"

In unison the children chimed in, "No you didn't Mom!"

"And..." Remy crowed triumphantly, "You gave us a sound bite, 'We're all immigrants'! I can see that being used over and over!"

Rachiel and Remy tipped their glasses in a toast and the children ran up to bed excitedly. They couldn't believe it, their parents were celebrities!

Remy was working in his den the next day pouring over e-mails and jotting down notes when the phone rang.

He picked up the receiver on his desk.

"Hello, Remy Gayo speaking."

A smooth, professional voice was on the other end. "Mr. Gayo, you don't know me but my name is Walter Hobbs."

Remy feigned interest. "Hello Mr. Hobbs, what can I do for you?"

"Mr. Gayo, I have been observing your campaign with interest. I, at one time, was a campaign manager for John Little, the former State Congressman."

Remy smiled and held the phone a little more firmly. "Well, thank you, I think. But, I'm not running for State Congress."

"I realize that. However, can I ask you why not?"

Remy paused and thought about it. "Well, I really don't have the money to do so. I also figured that I would start on a smaller level like the Party Chairman told me to do."

Hobbs paused dramatically on the other line. "Mr. Gayo, they told you that because they don't want to upset their status quo. You would represent new blood and that is not what they want. How about if I was to tell you, that your, um.., rather unconventional message is actually gaining momentum, and it's making a lot of people nervous?"

Remy smiled to himself and felt almost embarrassed and newly rejuvenated. He didn't know this Hobbs but he also had a feeling as though he felt like he was being set up. Remy decided to test Hobbs.

"How about if I told you and your kind, 'I told you so?' I have been ridiculed and chastised in the press for my message. And, do you know what has happened despite their attempts to discredit me? I've gained momentum and support. There are an awful lot of people who are in my position and have the feelings that I do."

"So I'm beginning to see. Say, do you have time to sit down and talk a bit?"

"If you're legit and truly care about my campaign, I guess so. But, I'll be up front with you, I don't have the means to pay you if that's what you're looking for."

"I realize that fact as much. Look, I'm pretty well set with my lobbying firm and I am legitimate. It's not often that I encounter a man with a growing contingent like yourself. But I'd like to sit with you and offer you a proposal."

"Fine, it's your time Hobbs. Where and when?"

"How about this afternoon? Over at Luna's Bistro?"

"Sounds good. See you then."

As he approached the restaurant in his car Remy realized that while he never really spent any time in the city proper, it had a personality all its own. Looking upwards as he exited his car he noticed the high rise buildings that shaped the landscape. Although Rochester didn't have as many high-rises as other cities, it seemed to have just enough to give it the character of a major city. In addition while the buildings looked impressive, they weren't too intrusive upon the skyline like in other cities. They allowed Rochester the high-tech personality it was known for.

Remy walked into the small restaurant located off of Jay Street in the city. Nestled in one of the older areas of the city, it had become an institution of Italian food in the city. With a menu as timeless as the building it was situated in it had a time capsule feel to it.

Directly in front of him to the right was the bar area. The brass railings on the upper edge and the foot of the bar exterior were well worn and exposed their age like a distinguished gentleman. The scratches, nicks and dents only served to accent the character that the rails had. Similarly, the surfaces of the bar revealed character. The heavy finished cherry wood panels were a halcyon of days gone by.

The cherry wood was a traditional material that just wasn't used in new-builds anymore. It was an understated elegance that sadly just didn't exist in most establishments of the current age.

To the left of the bar area was a series of small tables and at the rear of the bar area was the main seating area. As Remy looked around some of the lunch patrons started murmuring and pointing in recognition of Remy's television news appearances. Finally, a large, imposing man walked over towards Remy from the bar area where he was leaning.

As he approached, Remy looked the man up and down with a quick study to size him up. Well dressed, yet in a disheveled manner, the man stood about five feet eleven inches tall and weighed close to three hundred pounds. His tailored shoes were scuffed on the tops, a clear indication of his carelessness and disregard for the price of the fine leather accoutrements.

"Mr. Gayo! How are you!" the large man thrust his comparatively enormous hand out towards Remy's hand. Remy looked the imposing figure up and down and finally stopped at the man's thinning hair that was parted on the right to cover the gradually increasing bald spot.

"Mr. Hobbs, I presume?"

"Yes, yes, nice to meet you Remy, may I call you Remy?"

Remy smirked, he thought of that old joke "May I call you John? Only if I can call you ass-kisser" but, he thought better of it.

"That's fine, Mr. Hobbs"

"Walter, please. Well, shall we?" Hobbs motioned over to the entrance to the large seating area.

Remy nodded and followed Hobbs to the dining area. As he entered the main dining area a few diners stopped and looked up watching the two men entered the area. Remy and Walter took a seat at a round table towards the rear of the room. Hobbs resumed speaking as he took his seat.

"So, Remy. I have to admit, I've been in this business a long time. I've run a lot of campaigns for a lot of different people. And, I have to tell you, you're one of the rare ones. Not only do people support your message but I get the sense that they generally like and relate to you."

Remy smiled. "Well, that's flattering. However, you mentioned to me on the phone about having me changing the direction of my campaign."

Before Hobbs could answer, a middle-aged man approached Remy from a nearby table.

"Excuse me, Mr. Gayo? I don't mean to intrude but I would just like to say how much I and my family support you and your quest for public office."

Remy nodded courteously at the man and proceeded to stand up.

The man shook his head and motioned towards Remy. "Oh, please don't stand. I apologize for bothering you. I just wanted you to know that you're speaking for many of us."

Hobbs grinned ear to ear and nodded to Remy. Remy extended his hand and shook the visitor's hand. "Sir, thank you. Thank you very much. With your vote I aim to let our voice be heard beyond our town."

"I'm sure you will, sir. We, I mean all of us, are pulling for you!" The gentleman slightly bowed as he shook Remy's hand again and went back to his seat. Remy sat back down and looked at Hobbs.

Hobbs couldn't contain himself any longer. "My boy, see? I told you? You have something that most candidates can only dream of. You actually create excitement among people. You can make a difference! So, instead of talking you into it, just let me do it. If we take your message national you're a shoe in to become a Congressman!"

Remy shook his head. "Walter, I appreciate what you're telling me. But, I don't want to run for Congress just to suit your needs and ego. I have a responsibility towards my public. And I certainly can't abandon them now."

Hobbs smiled and placed his hand over Remy's. "Remy, don't you see? You will be able to serve your public better and more efficiently on a grander scale!"

The waiter came over and asked to take their order. The waiter took Walter's order first and then turned to Remy. When Remy looked up, the waiter smiled in recognition.

"Oh, Mr. Gayo! So nice to meet you! What can I get you sir?"

Remy scanned the menu quickly. "I'll have an iced tea and ... tripe! I'll have some tripe." Remy's thoughts wandered back to when his mother would make the dish with such careful devotion. Tripe, while disgusting on a first thought of the dish, was one of those peasant foods that took so much time to create that it was actually a comfort food. And, to Remy, the dish brought out many memories and good feelings. To actually find it on a menu, a diner knew that they were in a true ethnic eatery.

The waiter grinned ear-to-ear.

"Fantastic, Mr. Gayo. I'll get your orders out right away!"

Hobbs smiled again as Remy shook his head in disbelief. During their lunch Hobbs laid out the pros to Remy accepting his offer.

Remy listened intently and pondered everything that Hobbs threw at him. When they were finished, the waiter came over to ask if they wanted anything else.

"No, thank you, just the check please." Remy stated.

The waiter announced proudly. "No sir, it's on us. The owner would like you to know that we wish you the best and we look forward to the upcoming election. Also, if there is anything we can do for you let us know. You know, use the place as meeting area or such."

Remy nodded and thanked the young man profusely but insisted on paying. After a lengthy debate Remy convinced the waiter that if he accepted a free lunch that he would be just like the politicians he was running against. After Remy had paid for the lunch, Hobbs motioned for the two of them to get up.

Remy went home with a lot to think about. He scratched out on a legal pad the pros and cons to entering a bigger race. A lot of what Hobbs had said made sense. He would be able to help more people if he entered and won the larger race. Actually, he had begun to notice, before Hobbs said it, that the smaller races were comprised of cliques and special groups which only served a select few in the community. Entering the Congressional race would expose him to a larger stage. After discussing it with Rachiel he determined that he would do it.

Before Remy knew it, Hobbs took over his campaign and he was running for Congress in the 28th district. It all happened so fast, Remy didn't have time to literally catch his breath.

Suddenly, instead of Remy doing all the work he had a full staff at his disposal. Hobbs used his contacts and influences to roll the campaign forward. Fund raising was going through the roof and, suddenly, Remy didn't have to scrimp. Hobbs put him on a salary and set up a PAC in his name in order to funnel funds through. The PAC was called 'The Reality Fund,' a clear dismissal to the current White House resident's original PAC that he, himself had set up. Money poured into the PAC and both Remy and Walter were surprised at the number of businesses that were contributing.

Of course, as a late entry there was a lot of work to do but Remy was up for it. In fact, for the first time in a long time, probably in his life, except when he wanted to marry Rachiel, Remy was determined to see this project through.

Unfortunately, the big problem was the fact that they entered the race a little late. The amount of work it took to get caught up was seemingly almost insurmountable. If he didn't have the staff provided for him he would find it impossible to run a campaign of such magnitude.

Remy came home late as was becoming the usual occurrence one night. His hours were getting longer as the campaign gained momentum and he was busy constantly. And, as usual, Rachiel was waiting for him at the kitchen table.

"So, how did it go today?"

Remy walked in, loosened his tie, bent down to kiss his wife and then sat down himself.

"Good, tiring, but good. What are you still doing up? It's after 11."

Rachiel smiled at Remy, got up and poured two glasses of wine for each of them.

"Well, what else was I going to do? I'd feel funny drinking wine and eating biscotti alone!"

Remy smiled, "Oh, so that's it. You don't want to be known as an old lush!"

"I'll give you a lush!" Rachiel pretended to swing the bottle at Remy. "So, what's up?"

Remy took a sip of his wine. "I can't believe this"

"Believe what?"

"All of this. My gosh. Our fund raising has been through the roof, the support has been building, and now they want me to give a campaign speech. Who could have thought of all of this?" Remy shook his head in disbelief yet smiled ear-to-ear like the Cheshire cat.

Rachiel also grinned ear-to-ear, "I knew you could do this. In fact, I don't know how to say this.." she hesitated as she spoke.

Remy looked into Rachiel's eyes. "What? You mad at me?"

Rachiel laughed nervously and stood up and turned towards the sink as she continued talking to her husband. "No, silly. Absolutely not! I just want to tell you... Well… how proud I am of you." she hesitated saying those words hoping not to offend her husband.

"Proud? You weren't proud of me before?"

Rachiel turned around to face Remy but continued looking down towards the floor. 'Sigh' "No, I don't mean it that way. It's just that… It, you.. You always had it in you! You just didn't app…."

Remy sipped his wine and leaned back in his chair admonished. "Apply myself, right?" He finished Rachiel's sentence for her.

Rachiel nervously continued looked down at the floor. "Well, I don't mean it..."

Remy interrupted her with a shh-ing motion. "Look, I know. My mom used to tell me the same thing. And you know what?" He took a deep breath as he sat forward in the chair. "You're right. You know what? You're right. I guess I just never realized how much I didn't apply myself until now."

Rachiel took a seat and grasped her husband's hand across the counter. "Well, Rem, remember what your grandfather used to say."

Remy smiled broadly. "What? What was that?"

"A man's true character comes with how he handles adversity."

"I thought that was your dad who said that."

"No, it was your grandfather."

"Whatever, between my grandpa, dad, and your dad, they could have filled a book with their sayings."

"True, but, you have to admit, many of them are true"

"Yeah, I know, now I see it. Back then, I didn't. I was too busy thinking that they were full of shit."

Rachiel chuckled "Yeah, like how Sari and Angela think about you."

Remy stood up walked around the kitchen island to his wife and gave Rachiel a big hug. He sat back down in Rachiel's chair facing the chair back and looked up at his wife.

Rachiel could sense that something was on Remy's mind. "Well, what? What is it?"

Remy took a breath before he answered. "They want me to give a speech like I told you earlier. What am I going to do?"

"Well, that comes with the territory, doesn't it?"

"Yeah, I guess it does. But, here's the thing."

"Yes?"

"They said that they're going to have someone write it for me. I don't think that I want that. I started this; it should be my words, shouldn't it?"

Rachiel thought about it. "You're right. But, Rem, no offense, but what do you know about speeches?"

Remy nodded in acknowledgment. "Well, honestly, what did I know about running for office?"

Rachiel smiled, "True, true. But, I guess, where would you start?"

"I don't know, Rach. But it should be my words. Not someone else's, made to look like mine."

Rachiel smiled again. "Well, I could run to the library and get you a few books on speech-writing."

Remy smiled, "Hey, yeah. I didn't think about that!"

"And, you can probably get on the internet and read some of the more famous speeches and just simply plagiarize them!"

"You're right, Rach. I'll get on it, you loveable jerk!"

Rachiel smiled at her husband again. "Well, you better get busy."

Remy stared at Rachiel and just about ran over to hug her again. "Baby, you're the greatest"

"Gee, thanks Ralph, just don't threaten to send me to the moon or, so help me, I'll belt you one!"

The two of them started laughing so hard tears were in their eyes.

Chapter 30

As Remy's campaign gathered steam, the pressure on him started to increase exponentially. He worked on his speech every day in between his appearances and press releases. His home office was filled with books on writing from the library and his computer screen was filled with open windows on past speeches by historical figures. He would begin by copying, verbatim, passages from the prior speeches. This repetitive learning technique helped him to understand the structure and nuances of well written speeches. He had completed two and a half pages so far and was closing in on finishing his own speech when the phone rang.

"Hello, Remy Gayo speaking"

"Remy, Walter here."

"Yeah, Walt, what's up? Look, I'm just about finished with..."

"Rem, this isn't about the speech. I've got something else for you."

Remy paused a bit. How much more did he have to do for this? He never, in his wildest dreams, realized that running for office was this involved. My gosh, looking at the politicians on television he had no idea how much they really did. On the surface it looked as though all they did was float in and out of venues and television shows and give their opinions, inane as they were (he thought), on the various 'hot' topics as determined by the press and then went back to their posh homes and country clubs.

Remy audibly sighed, "What do you have now, Walt?"

Walter chuckled, "Hey, I warned you before we started that this would be a lot of work! Anyway... Remy, my boy, the time has come."

"The time has come for what?"

This time it was Walter's turn to take an audible breath. "Remy, you do know that we are getting under our opponents' skins."

"Yeah, I know that. Look how they ambushed Rachiel!"

"That's right! Good job by her, by the way. Now, you know that due to your success they're ramping up some negative ads on you."

Remy smirked, "Well, I assumed as much. What do you think they're going to hit me with this time?"

"Well, I don't know for certain but, this is what I think. Ready?"

Remy took a seat at his desk and grabbed a pen and a pad. "Ready."

"Okay, now, I'm going to speak on what I would go after, if I was in their position. Now, remember, don't take any of this personal or to heart."

"I'll try not to, I'm learning that, the hard way unfortunately, but I am learning. So, shoot."

"All right. First, they're going to attack your lack of credibility and experience. That's first and foremost. They are going to try and build the case that you would be ineffective in your first year while you learn the ropes. They're also going to go after your lack of a college degree. They're going to make it sound as though you're a quitter and you don't have the discipline to complete anything."

"Well, I could see that. But, that happened over twenty years ago! Would that be relevant?"

"Remy, my boy, in politics everything is timeless and nearly everything is fair game. Remember that."

Remy scribbled down his notes about the issue. "Okay, so I'm going to have to come up with an answer to that. Yet, you know, many people my age never..."

Hobbs cut him off. "That's great, think about that. Now, next they're going to try and label you an enemy of the underclass. They've already started with the racism innuendos and the anti-immigrant stance."

"Yeah, I caught that."

"Okay… but that's all right. As long as you don't lose your composure we can build on that and expand your base."

"Yeah, but, let's be honest Hobbs, why would I want the votes of people who think like that?"

"Be careful, Remy you don't want to alienate anybody. And, here's why. Because, MOST people don't think like that, you're right. Your opposition and their media allies will have you think that they do though. However, the reality is that very few people think in those extremes and that the ones on the fence, the ones in the middle, will vote for the candidate that doesn't sound like an ass. How do you think the current President got elected? On his vaunted ability to tell the truth? I think not!"

Remy laughed aloud and then paused on the other end while he was writing down notes. "So, what else?"

"Well, those are the big points that they can probably go after you with. Yet, the nice thing is that you lived such an innocuous life, that there really aren't a lot of other items that they can choose to pick on you about. Trust me. I did my research before I contacted you for the first time."

Remy chuckled aloud. "Well, I guess there's something to be said for normal and boring!"

"Remy, trust me; there is nothing boring about you now. Now, on to my original point, I think it's time for you to debate your opponent."

Remy froze. "Walter, but my speech isn't ready!"

Hobbs continued, "Remy, this is perfect timing. First, we have this debate, then the public will be intrigued by you and your speech will attract more listeners than you ever thought!"

Walter began to sense Remy's trepidation over the phone line. "Remy, we have to do this. We're gaining so much in momentum that it's something I've never seen before!"

"Walter, how am I supposed to handle this? I mean, I've never done a debate. Not even in High School!"

Walter smiled. "It's Ok. We'll coach you through it! Trust me, not even the current President knew how to debate before his campaign. They staged mock debates for him until he got comfortable doing them. That is just like how we're going to coach you through yours."

Remy shook his head. But, then he realized, he started this ride, and it was his obligation to see it through to the end. Remy sighed audibly, "All right. Well, you've got your work cut out for you. When do we start?"

"Show up at the campaign office tomorrow and I'll have everything in the works!"

When Remy arrived at the office, Hobbs did indeed have everything ready. Hobbs had contacted Remy's opponent and arranged the debate for the following Wednesday evening. He had also arranged for the local and district television stations to cover it.

Hobbs decided not to tell Remy about the number of news outlets that would be covering the event though. "The man is nervous as it is. The smaller I can make the debate seem the better for him," he thought.

Hobbs went all out for the training session. He had two podiums brought into the room along with chairs and a center area for the moderator. The piece de resistance was the appearance of his debate partner. Hobbs actually had the campaign worker styled and dressed to appear as his debate opponent, Elizabeth Holtman.

Elizabeth Holtman was a slightly experienced congresswoman who represented the 28th district in New York State currently. Smart, intelligent, and savvy, she was the daughter of Hyman Holtman, the 'Loganberry King' in Western New York. Her father had started his business as a young man providing beverages to local delis. From there, he grew the business into one of the largest beverage distributorships in the country. His company actually supplied the majority of the libations that were available in kosher delis across the country. From his humble beginnings he had built a strong and viable company.

His daughter, Elizabeth, while enjoying a privileged lifestyle, still worked hard for everything she had. Her Father, while he doted on her, decided to instill a work ethic within his daughter. He made her work for everything she got, including her college education. Growing up she didn't have an allowance, and, in fact, the only way she earned any spending money was accompanying her father to work where she performed small jobs. When she graduated from New York University she passed the bar exam on her first attempt. She had chosen NYU over schools such as Yale and Georgetown because she wanted to prove to herself that she could go to a lower profile school and still be effective.

And, effective she was. After graduation she obtained a position with a law firm in New York and quickly proceeded up the rungs of the ladder. By the time she was thirty years old she had achieved partner status. Yet, in spite of her success in life at a young age, she still wanted to do more. After her marriage to a prominent cardiologist, Jonathan Ensenberger, she started whispering in her husband's ear about the possibilities of her running for political office.

Additionally, as fate would have it, Rochester General Hospital had taken upon itself to expand and market its Cardiology department. 'The Northeast's best heart hospital' their ads trumpeted. Jonathan, looking to assist his wife, and also forward his career, made inquiries at RGH and eventually accepted a position as Chief Cardiologist there. This opened the door for Elizabeth to start her own firm and begin her pursuit of politics.

Elizabeth ran for the 25th district seat eight years ago. Meticulous and precise, she employed a research firm to plan her new venture. She found out that the polling research showed an opening in the political landscape. The incumbent, John Traverse, had held the office for the past 15 years. In two of those elections he essentially ran unopposed on the Republican ticket. However, as safe as he was in the past, the political climate was changing across the country. The conservatives were falling out of favor among the masses and the populace was starting to lean left once again.

Elizabeth realized then that if she was going to enter politics, now was the time. Although her professional and personal feelings leant themselves more towards the other side, her ticket to success was to present herself on the Democratic ticket. And, she did that, adeptly. When Traverse's people brought up her upbringing and husband's profession the Democratic Party's press contacts adeptly countered any disparaging stories. She adopted all of the latest party lines as her own and made sure that of all her photo ops were with the right causes. Soon enough, she was the portrait of the Democratic Party in her district.

Remy worked hard at the debate practice. His practice opponent pulled out questions about racism, bigotry and his perceived disingenuity towards the plight of the poor. At first, Remy answered angrily and defensively. Slowly, Hobbs taught him to keep his emotions in check and to answer all questions, regardless of his personal preference, in a tight, moderated manner. Remy wasn't feeling any more comfortable about the act of a debate but his behavior pattern in dealing with verbal adversity definitely grew.

The day of the debate arrived. Despite Hobbs' best efforts to downplay it, Remy discovered that the debate was a big event. Not only was the local television network carrying it, but the cable news network and also QNN.

Remy's campaign had started to strike a national chord. The networks realized and embraced that this was a true 'little' guy against the established professionals' type of story. It was the kind of story that many readers and viewers could relate to and were anxious to follow. While the media outlets didn't feel that Remy could win, it proved for good copy. The public loved David and Goliath stories, especially in politics.

Remy winced a little when the make-up artists touched him up for the debate. "Geesh, is this what Rach does every morning?" he thought as he sat in the padded chair as the make-up artist shaped his eyebrows, tweezed hair he didn't even know he had, and colored his face.

Remy walked towards the podium steeling himself for the debate. He had never done anything like this before but, like the art of running for office he reminded himself again, he figured if they could do it he could do it. He glanced nervously at the lights, the stage, and the general surroundings of cables and cameras that were never displayed on the television. The producer instructed Remy where to stand. There was a tape designed 'X' behind the podium. The producer instructed Remy that it was best that he stayed on that particular spot.

The moderator motioned to the producer and gave the participants and the audience the debate rules. There would be one minute, 45 seconds to answer the questions and the candidate would have to defer to the opponent politely and quickly.

Just before the lights were ready to rise the moderator gave the two participants their final instructions. He then signaled and the participants got ready. Remy's opponent stood composed and confident while Remy felt a tinge of nervousness as he stood at his podium.

The moderator began the debate after the introductions and the debate rules were laid out. "First question, and I will direct it at Mr. Gayo first, then Ms. Holtman. Mr. Gayo, many citizens are concerned with what they see as excessive illegal immigration. Our borders are not patrolled as they should be and are open is the feeling of many detractors. You have leaned against immigration. So, what is your position on immigration? Should we enact tougher laws or alter the system?"

Remy looked at the moderator with an incredulous look on his face before he answered. Composing himself he presented his response. "Immigration is an important part of the American fabric. This great country was built on the backs of immigrants. We can't keep people out of our country, that isn't right. If they enter legally and honestly they can add to our social fabric. It's Illegal immigration that is the problem. What really needs to be done is to refocus and straighten out the immigration laws that have been twisted and ignored."

"Ms. Holtman?"

"Thank you. Illegal Immigration is a problem in our country that is said to be eroding the very core of our people by our political opponents. We need to repair the immigration laws so that no one in this country is penalized for being here regardless of how they entered. Amnesty and understanding is what is required. Mr. Gayo, due to his inexperience fails to see or realize this."

Remy shook his head and smirked. He was waiting for this type of attack.

"Rebuttal Mr. Gayo? You have 45 seconds."

"Ms. Holtman, where was your grandfather born?"

"Um… here in the United States."

"Ok, what is your ethnic background?"

"American, I guess. Why? What is your point?"

The moderator broke in, "Yes Mr. Gayo, your point. You are running out of time."

"My point is that according to your definition you are not 'American,' in fact, none of us truly are. The only ones that are, I do not see represented here. And that would be the Native Americans. You, Ms. Holden are of Polish/Jewish origin and you yourself are descended from immigrants who entered this country legally."
The moderator burst in.

"Mr. Gayo, you are getting off of the point. I will have to cease this question and move on to the next."

The audience started to buzz. Remy smirked at the podium.

Suddenly Ms. Holtman broke out with a statement. The words had struck her hard. "Now, see here, Mr. Gayo. I am an American, and I'm so impressed that you did research on my ethnic background."

Remy grinned, he had made her think and cause her to slightly lose her composure.

The moderator tried to move the debate forward but was visibly perturbed at Remy's tactics. He glanced through his notes and chose the next question. "This question is for Congresswoman Holtman. Ms. Holtman, what is your position on the growing sentiment of decreasing public aid money for the less fortunate?"

Remy smiled, yep, like Hobbs said, they're trying to make him look insensitive to the poor.

"The issue of the urban poor is a multi-faceted one. These people need programs and funding to help them succeed in our society. Many of them are just victims of draconian programs that need to be overhauled. What they need are increased opportunities at education and good housing which will help them rise above their lot. Not diminished programs which my opponent seems so enamored with."

Ms. Holtman's supporters clapped loudly.

"Mr. Gayo?"

"Thank you. If you give a man a fish, you feed him for a day, yet if you teach him to catch a fish, you do him a good turn. Contrary to popular, no, my detractors' belief, I have no ill towards the disenfranchised. I do believe that there should be programs to assist them. However, where I disagree with my opponent is the manner of assistance. What we need to do is to re-allocate the money that we use for programs and to turn them into jobs. Jobs are what people need, not handouts. If you give a person a job, you give them self-respect and self-reliance. And that goes much farther than merely giving them a handout."

Remy's proponents cheered loudly.

"Ms. Holtman, Rebuttal?" the moderator rolled his eyes at Remy as he addressed Elizabeth.

"Yes, well, Mr. Gayo. And just how do you intend to create such programs? It is evident that your complete lack of experience and your naiveté lead you to state such idealistic goals with neither the means of knowledge to make such statements into reality."

Remy took a deep breath and smirked. "Is this the way you debate? By ridiculing your opponent?"

The moderator burst in angrily.

"Mr. Gayo, your time is ended. Now, let's move onto the next question."

Remy couldn't believe what he was hearing. "No, I will not move on. This isn't right!"

Holtman chuckled. "I rest my case."

"Rest your case?!" Remy began to lose his composure. As the crowd cheered and booed at the same time, he looked towards Rachiel for support and as his eyes fell on her she shook her head as she mouthed the words "Don't give in to it." He closed his eyes and nodded.

The moderator attempted to regain control of the debate. "Now, let's move on shall we? Ms. Holtman, um.. rest assured that the management of this station are behind you."

Remy's head snapped quickly with that slip from the moderator. "Excuse me?"

"Mr. Gayo, let's move on please"

"No, we will not move on. Did you just say that your station supports my opponent? What is the use of this debate? To attempt to embarrass me?"

The moderator stared directly at Remy. "Mr. Gayo, we need to move this forum on. Our first two questions are finished. Our audience would like to see more than just those two topics especially the problem of immigration."

Remy shook his head once more. "Problem? It's only a problem because venues like yours have escalated it into a 'problem.' Perhaps if you reported accurately on stories it wouldn't be perceived as a 'problem.'

The moderator ignored Remy's speech and attempted to move on.

Remy decided to push forward as the audience started to rouse. He addressed his opponent first. "Ms. Holtman, it is public record that your father is known as the 'Loganberry King' among deli owners. Am I correct?"

Holtman answered but with a question in her voice as to the direction of this line of questioning. "Um... Yes. What of it?"

"Well, isn't it safe to say that you are the product of a legal immigrant businessman and that as a child you enjoyed the fruits of your father's hard work? Work that your father performed by himself without the assistance of others?"

"Yes, but..."

"Nothing more. It just doesn't seem to me that you are representing your upbringing honestly with many of the things that you say and the programs you represent. I, on the other hand, am rather proud of my Spanish-Italian roots."

The moderator broke in angrily. "Mr. Gayo. You are off of the subject. This is a debate, not a beratement!"

"Oh, excuse me, I didn't realize that I was upsetting you." he grinned.

The moderator adjusted his jacket and shook his head indignantly. "Mr. Gayo, you are not upsetting me, you are upsetting our viewers! Now, can we proceed with the debate?"

Remy smiled wickedly. "Absolutely, but, I have to ask. Are you that out of touch with your customers?"

"Sir, we don't have customers, we have viewers"

"That's what I mean, customers ARE viewers. You and your peers appear to have forgotten that."

"Mr. Gayo, can we move on to the debate?"

"I will. As soon as I get this off my chest. You people in the media seem to have forgotten that it is your job to report the news, not tilt it to your opinion and feelings on how things should be. You truly think that we, the public, are stupid and that we will swim in the current that you create!"

The audience broke out in a roar approvingly. The moderator looked around angrily as he attempted to regain control. "Now, see here, Mr. Gayo, this is supposed to be a debate. Not a venue for your personal agenda."

Remy gave the death stare to the moderator, took a deep breath, looked over at the audience and then Rachiel and continued. "This isn't MY personal agenda. This is the agenda of the people. Here's a news flash for you. What I'm saying is what the people truly feel. Not YOUR station's editorial mandate of what we're supposed to feel. So, allow me to reiterate, We, the people, are tired of being assumed for!"

With that, the room broke out in chaos. Even Remy's opponent's supporters joined out in cheers. Remy looked over to his opponent and noticed that even she was nodding her head in approval. The moderator looked over helplessly and angrily at the producer and made the cutting motion across his throat to kill the lights. Even that didn't quell the din in the room. Then, when Remy motioned for the room to quiet it slowly did.

The moderator scanned the room and gave the producer the thumbs up to continue. Yet, the damage had been done; the tone of the debate was changed from that moment on.

The next day the papers once again attempted to slaughter Remy. "Minor league pol uses debate as personal agenda," "Hitler Remy spouts own mantra," were some of the kinder ones. Remy read them and quickly put them out of his mind. He was onto something and he was becoming more determined to continue it.

<u>Chapter 31</u>

The hand of the diligent will rule, while the slothful will be put to forced labor.
Proverbs 12:24

Hobbs figured it perfectly. Although He wasn't pleased with Remy's wandering from the debate topics he couldn't argue with the support it garnered. The aftermath of the debate was deafening. Where the media thought that it would harm Remy's campaign, it actually served to strengthen and increase its support. Remy was right. There were an awful lot of people who felt the way he did. Yet, regardless of the impression he felt, he was still behind in the polls according to the press.

Remy called Hobbs on the phone nervously. "Walter, should I continue? All signs point to me losing."

Hobbs chuckled assuredly before he answered. "Remy, Remy, Remy, that's what the press does. The great American pastime, besides baseball, is to watch a popular person defeated. The press will purposely manipulate the polls to produce the results they want. That's how they build a story. People love to read about failure. Remember what they did to your wife? They led her with questions. That's how they conduct their polls. Don't worry. Our financial numbers speak otherwise!"

"What do you mean our financials? What are they showing?"

"Remy, my boy, we are out drawing our opponent by two to one! Do you know what that means?"

Remy really didn't. "So..."

"Trust me; people don't give money to losing causes. The money contribution tells us that the polls are crap. We aren't big enough to have corporations give to us. These are all small donations from individuals and families!"

"You're kidding me!"

"Remy, I never kid. Now, stop with this negative outlook and pick yourself up! The hard work is only just beginning!"

Remy's head swelled with the reality of it all. "Hard work? Just begin? What I have been doing since?" Remy thought to himself.

Remy still couldn't believe it. In a way, he felt as though he was purposely sabotaging his new career because he didn't think he deserved it.

Hobbs broke Remy's thoughts. "Now, I hope you have your speech ready. I scheduled you for tomorrow at the Veteran's Post in the town of Ontario at 1:00."

Remy stuttered with the reality of it. "W-w-ell, I think I'm ready."

Hobbs barked. "Either you are, or you aren't. And, if I know you by now, you will be!"

Hobbs' words struck a chord. In fact, he swore he heard Salvatore's voice delivering those words.

Tomorrow arrived with a rush to Remy. Before he had time to think about it, he awoke, got ready, grabbed his speech and was out the door.

Entering the Veteran's post in Ontario, New York, he smiled as he looked at the clean tile floors and the flags hanging on the walls. In the center of the open room was the bar where the usual gang sat and enjoyed their draft beers. Remy had seen quite a few of these as he was growing up when he accompanied his Father on occasion.

Remy smiled and greeted the bar patrons. One of them stood up animatedly and shook Remy's hand vigorously. He stood about six feet tall and had a slight stoop to his body making him appear shorter. The lines on his face and the color in his hair revealed that he was in his seventies, yet his enthusiastic voice displayed the youthfulness that still existed within him.

"It is a pleasure to meet you, Mr. Gayo!"

"Thank you. But, the pleasure is all mine, sir."

The old man grinned ear-to-ear. "I knew it! Didn't I tell you guys?" He looked at his bar companions.

The other fellows at the bar shook their heads in agreement towards Remy. A shorter and slightly younger gentleman spoke first.

"Yep, old Tim there hasn't stopped talking about you. He says that you're the last of the honest men."

Remy turned to him. "Well, thank you. I try."

Tim waved his arm animatedly. "No, you don't try. You do! I can tell, WE can tell." He gestured towards his bar mates as he continued.

"Let me tell you something! I can tell when a man is truthful. Hell, I learned that when I served my time in Korea."

The shorter man sighed as though he had heard this before in way too many different ways.

Tim took his seat at the bar and motioned Remy to join him. Remy took a seat and Tim gestured towards the bartender. A draft beer was presented in front of Remy. "I'm telling you. You're the real thing! I know that I'm going to vote for you!"

Remy looked at his beer consciously. Should he drink it before his speech? If he didn't, he would insult a possible voter. If he did he ran the risk of being labeled a drunk by the opposition. As he bounced those thoughts around in his head he began to realize that this was a part of being a politician.

Remy thought about it quickly. The hell with it, if he didn't share a swig with this man, he would be just as disingenuous as the rest of the politicians he was rallying against.

"Thank you, Tim. And, thank you for serving in Korea."

"Hell, it was my pleasure son. Besides, it's not like I had a choice. I was drafted!"

He let out a large laugh and the others seated at the bar joined him.

"How about you? Did you or your brood serve?"

Remy looked down as he answered. "No sir, not I. I mean, I tried. Heck, they drove me up to Buffalo for my physical even, but they told me I couldn't join due to my allergies." Remy paused, took a sip of his beer and continued, "But my dad served. He served in Korea!" Remy looked up quickly.

"He did? Well, good. He must have been a fine man!"

Remy felt a hand on his shoulder from the man to his left. "Son, there ain't no shame in not serving. Trust me, many a man in my era wouldn't have served if they didn't have to. The thing with you, your heart was there, and, in the long run that's all that counts."

Remy turned and nodded towards the man. "Um, thanks, Mr...."

"John, you can call me John. My father was Mr."

"Yeah, back in the stone ages!" Tim cut John off with his booming laugh.

John smiled, "Well, if you listen to that youngster, then what does he know? He served in a 'Police Action'; I served in the real war!"

"Whoaa... Here we go! Remy, you better run now son otherwise you'll be smelling like the inside of a horse barn by the time he's done!"

Remy took this as his cue to get up. "Fellows, I can't say enough, how great it was to talk to you all. But, I have to go campaign now." He threw a twenty on the bar and motioned to the bartender. "That enough for everyone?"

The bartender smiled. "Remy, it's enough for all night for these guys. I only charge these old mallards fifty cents a draft. And, trust me; they're too cheap to go for anything else!"

Tim raised his glass to Remy in a mock toast. "Mallard? Listen to him; he thinks he's hot stuff because he's younger than us. He served in 'Nam. Ain't he special?"

"Yeah, and there were no ticker tape parades when I came home!"

Tim and John laughed and said in unison, "Stop you're whining, baby. Waaahhh, they don't like me!"

Tim continued, "Just a bunch of teat sucking Mama's boys we're protesting them. Damn group of spoiled, unappreciative brats. They forget, if it wasn't for us they wouldn't have a place to protest. Of course, they would be the ones licking the Emperor's boot heels, bunch of pansy assed..."

John cut him off. "Ok, big guy. This is about Remy, not those morons."

Now it was Remy's turn to laugh. And laugh he did. He placed a hand on both men's shoulders. "Guys, thanks. It was great talking with you." Remy waved goodbye as he made his way into the meeting room.

"Good luck, kid. You've got my vote!" Tim yelled towards Remy.

"What a good kid." John said as he settled into his stool and brought his glass to his lips.

Remy stood in front of the crowd. Walter had arranged the audience, the venue, and the time. Press releases were sent out to every news outlet in the city.

Hobbs also sent out releases to the major news networks. Normally they would ignore, or give limited coverage to a small race, but Walter and the networks at large felt something unique about Remy. For the first time in his political career Hobbs felt as though he was looking at the original article, not a professional politician.

Although Walter was quietly unhappy that Remy chose to write his own speech, he appreciated the effort that Remy put into it. But, he was also concerned. Remy hadn't shared the speech with him. He hoped that it was polished enough to be acceptable to the crowd and to the media. Of course, to many of Remy's supporters it didn't matter. This was truly a grass roots campaign as it used to be done before the government became an institution. This was a throwback to the days of men leaving their farms, serving the people for two to four years and then going back to their farms.

As Hobbs began to run his polling process he saw it build momentum also. Remy was gaining an incredible amount of support in an extremely short period of time.

As Remy walked up to the dais he scanned the crowd. It was bigger than he expected. People had caught wind of the upcoming speech and found their way to attend it. Many of the audience had taken an extended lunch or just time off to find their way to the speech. After the debate debacle they were not going to wait for the news outlets to report the speech to them. They wanted to witness every word themselves. In fact, some of the audience had entered with their phones and tablets set to record the speech for posting onto MyTube.

His core supporters wanted to make sure that Remy's message was conveyed as it should be. Even Walter himself shook his head in amazement, with a smile ear-to-ear, at the number of people in attendance.

Remy cleared his throat, he looked over at Rachiel who was seated to the left of the stage and shuffled his papers. He scanned the crowd once again and noticed his new companions Tim, John, and the rest of the bar patrons in the very rear of the room, glasses in hand.

Remy took a deep breath, said a silent prayer and smiled before he started. "Hello, thank you for coming. I will make this brief. At least I think it will be. But, bear with me; this is the first speech I have ever written, let alone given!"

The crowd broke out in applause and then waited. People were whispering to each other as he started to speak.

"Of the people, for the people, and, by the people. Those words stand for the basic principles under which this country was built. But, they are words that somehow have been forgotten, and perhaps ignored, as time has marched on and our country has grown."

"As a second generation American, those words hold great value to me. My grandparents, as they came over here from Europe, embraced the ideals and hopes of this country and built lives here. Lives that they were not able to obtain in their native lands."

"They worked hard, bought homes, and raised families with good moral values here, in this country. In addition to those benefits they were also able to practice their own religions without fear of oppression. This country was the American dream to them and they supported each other and helped build the communities that have lasted and we know today. They were the backbone of this great country of ours."

Remy paused.

"But, now. Now the message has begun to get tarnished. What was once the backbone of this country has unfortunately turned into a forgotten segment of the country."

The crowd clapped. Remy paused, smiled at the crowd and continued. "Instead, what has happened is that the elite and the designer poor have all but squeezed us, the middle class, out. Now, although we pay the taxes and maintain the communities, we are treated as a bother by the very people we support."

The crowd broke out in a large applause. Remy smiled again but altered his demeanor to deliver the next segment.

"When the CEO of a corporation makes a mistake they aren't hurt. Sure, they lose their job, but more times than not they are given a golden parachute. Millions of dollars and other options are given to them for their failure. And, I ask why? Their failures affect and destroy hundreds and even thousands of lives, yet they are taken care of. Again, why?"

The crowd roared louder at this. Remy nodded and continued. Hobbs was smiling ear-to-ear, the boy had done it; he was starting to think.

"On top of that, when a terminally lazy person determines that they are not going to work, they manipulate the system, the system that we finance, for housing, food, clothing, phones, and the such. A system that we, as compassionate people, have put into place to assist the less fortunate. Yet, thanks to our indifference and apathy, the system has become manipulated by the unscrupulous. While at the same time, those of us who truly need the programs and support, the mentally ill, the elderly, the sick, they get nothing. No help. Or, if they do, they have to leap through so much red tape, that many give up before they receive it."

Loud cheering and clapping continued. Hobbs looked on nervously. "Where is he going?" Remy continued with a stern look.

"And, who pays these groups? Who supports these groups? We do. We, the ones that when we lose our jobs are given nothing but what we put into the system. If one of us determines that we don't want to work we are turned away because we did the right thing and worked and saved."

The crowd fell silent and Remy took advantage of the dramatic pause. He raised his eyes as though he was looking into the eyes of each and every attendee. "It isn't right."

Hobbs grabbed his handkerchief and wiped his brow.

"This country was built on the blood and sweat of our forefathers. What was once a country built on hard work and dreams has become a country of takers. And, make no mistake; there is no difference from the elite rich or the designer poor. They are one and the same, two groups who do not contribute and yet have their hands out to take what we earn, what we have produced, what we have toiled for!"

The crowd exploded in applause. As Remy looked up he noticed that the room had filled with even more people. Phones and tablets were held up to record every word. Remy thought about this quickly. Where before he would have been nervous about giving a speech he was suddenly energized. In fact, he seemed to feed off of the energy of the crowd. Remy scanned the room and focused for his next delivery.

"People. We, the people, need to take this country back. We need to show this country that we are the backbone. That if it wasn't for us there would be no programs for the rich or the poor. We need to show them that WE are the people. The people who are of the people, for the people, and by the people!"

The crowd erupted into a deafening roar. Remy paused and then continued. Hobbs was beside himself. This was the real thing after all.

Remy closed his eyes and continued after he waited for the noise to die down. He raised his right arm in a sweeping motion with his right hand open and extended.

"Now, will we fix things overnight? Absolutely not. It took years to erode into this and it will take years to fix it. But, can we fix it, you ask? Absolutely. We can fix it because we are the ones who built it, and we are the ones who let it get to this point."

The crowd stood silent.

"Yes, we allowed it to get to this point! Us! For years, we, the people, sat in indifference and left things up to others to take care of. We became so self absorbed within our own lives. What did we care that a CEO made so much or that a lazy person wanted to take from the system? Not us. There was enough to go around. We still had our boats, our second and third cars, and our other toys and whatever else we wanted. It didn't matter to us what others had because we had our own. Now, that time is no longer."

"Now, we don't have the jobs or the income to buy our toys. Now we don't even have enough to pay our mortgages or buy food or gas. Now, the tide has turned and we have no one to blame but ourselves."

The crowd started cheering nervously. Remy's words began to hit home.

"No, NOW is the time when we take charge again. NOW is the time that we re-assert ourselves as THE driving force in this country. We need to elect people that are of us and about us. Not these out of touch elitists that we keep electing. We don't need more of what we have presently; we need real people who represent us, regardless of party affiliation."

Remy delivered this with a tremendous emotion in his voice. The crowd sensed it and roared loudly. As he glanced around the room he noticed his new bar buddies raising their glasses towards him. He continued.

"And after we do that, then we need to begin with real reforms. Not lobbyist driven reforms instituted by the political and business elite. We need real reform generated by us, the biggest lobby in the country! People! You DO realize that the middle, working class comprises almost 90% of this country, don't you! And yet we allow ourselves to be continually bullied by the minority classes. Yes, the rich and the poor!"

With that, the room erupted into a huge applause.

"We need to hold the elite accountable. If they crash a business due to their ineptness we need them to walk away with nothing. Their salaries need to be given to the employees that they damaged. Not from the taxes that those employees paid into!"

Remy paused again for dramatic effect and then continued. "We also need social services reform. We need to have these people contribute to society. Everyone can do something. It isn't their fault. My grandfather, a man that worked hard every day of his life, once said that a man that just receives with no effort given has no appreciation for what he receives. Yet we can't blame them for their attitude. Because, if we really examine it, we, the people, have given them that attitude. Haven't we?"

The crowd burst into screaming. Remy waited until they quieted again.

"And, the biggest thing is that we need to get back to being supportive of each other. This country wasn't built on separatism, it was built with cooperation, amongst all of us, rich , poor, dark, light, and such all! There was a time when the other countries in the world were scared of us. Because there was nothing scarier than the united people of the United States! We need to unify and take back our government to a government for, by, and of the people! It is only then that we can bring our country and ourselves back to the respect and prominence that we deserve!"

The crowd erupted again. In fact, some of the reporters even applauded. Remy had hit the nerve that before no one was brave enough to say.

"With that, I will conclude my speech and once again thank everyone for their support. And remember, We can do it! But, it's going to take time. Once again, we let it get this way, now it's up to us to bring it back! God Bless!"

As he watched the crowd burst into an almost unforeseen frenzy, Walter shook his head in disbelief. This had really turned into something.

Chapter 32

You will forget your misery; you will remember it as waters that have passed away. (Job 11:16)

As it became to be expected, the Press hit hard that night and the following day about the speech.

'Gayo's racist rant hits nerve with people,' 'Green Pol hopeful insults everyone with speech,' were some of the headlines screaming out on the internet and newsstands. However, team Gayo was prepared.

Before the speech was ever orated, Walter had the campaign ready everything in anticipation. Immediately after the speech was given, the entire transcript was available on the campaign's website, Mybook page, and every other media outlet available.

Walter had aides monitor Chirper and answer immediately any questions and squelch any derogatory rumors and half-truths. The speech served its purpose, it made Remy a household name.

Remy himself couldn't believe the impact it had. He was mobbed everywhere he went. His front lawn was literally a camp for reporters to try and gain his reaction.

Remy had begun to get quite adept at answering reporters' questions and actually began to have fun with it.

"Mr. Gayo, are you to say that the poor are poor because of their own doing?"

"No, I never said that. Look, as Jesus said, there will be poor always, but it's up to us to help them. Giving people handouts doesn't help them, it only serves to embarrass them more. A lack of dignity hurts a man more than anything."

Remy smiled to himself, he had purposely baited the news media with the mention of Jesus. The press loved to label people as religious 'fanatics'. Of course, the joke was on them; over 75% of the country was of Christian faith, another largely forgotten 'lobby' that had the ability to disrupt.

Another reporter asked the next question. "Mr. Gayo, when you told everyone to unify and go after the government, does that mean you condone revolutionary violence?"

Remy smirked at the leading of the question. He was becoming wise to the reporter's tactics. "No, did I say that? What I said is that we have the government and the structure so that we can be heard in this country. I, in no uncertain terms, implied violence. If you got that from my words then you obviously need professional help or you need to stop drinking to excess every night bemoaning your poor career choice. What I am saying is we need to use our voting process to institute change, not idleness like we practiced before."

The reporter was angered at Remy's response. Politicians aren't supposed to take personal shots at a reporter! It wasn't in the rules!

Another reporter attempted to ambush Remy. "Mr. Gayo, are you saying that all business owners are evil?"

Remy chuckled at this one. "No. Business owners are an important element of this country. They employ people and they pay taxes. I never said anyone was evil. If you listened to the speech you would clearly know that what I don't support is men taking advantage of the system and prospering off of the backs of the workers. There are many business owners who are good, caring people. Just like those they employ."

"Mr. Gayo, what do you mean by designer poor? Are you saying that they aren't really poor?"

"No, like I said before, there will be poor always. What I mean by designer poor are the people who, for whatever reason, have chosen to be poor so that they can take advantage of the system. Therefore, they are poor by design, not circumstance."

It went on like this over and over. Remy began to grow weary of this line of questioning. However, he realized that it was a part of the job and he was growing better at it.

A day later, Hobbs called animatedly. Even more so than he usually was. The phone rang at Remy's desk.

"Hello, Remy Gayo here."

"Remy, my boy. How are you?"

"Hobbs. I'm fine, thank you. What's up?"

"You won't believe it!"

Remy shrugged his shoulders. "What? Did I win the election by default?"

Hobbs chuckled. "If only, if only. No, you do realize that it is only two weeks before the election? Right?"

"Yes Walter, I do. What of it?"

"Well, we have a huge opportunity!"

Remy shook his head even though Hobbs couldn't see it. "Walter, what?"

"Remy, you have been invited to be on the Wilma Opine Show!"

Remy paused. "You're kidding me, right?"

"No, my boy. I'm dead serious."

"But why? Walter, don't you understand? She's going to crucify me! She is as Democratic leaning as they get! Heck, our current President won, I feel, in large part to her endorsement of him!"

Walter thought a little about this and continued.

"Remy, don't you realize what this can do for you? You'd be on one of the most influential and popular shows in the world. Even if she blasts you, think about the audience that you can get your message through! If you convert five percent of them, that's a tremendous amount!"

"But what if she embarrasses me?"

"Remy, haven't you taught yourself anything? All publicity, good or bad, is good!"

Remy thought hard. Hobbs made sense. Yet, he definitely didn't want to make himself look like a fool. "Walter, what good is appearing on her show going to do for me? She's in Manhattan for Pete's sake."

"Yes, Remy, and her show is syndicated across the country. Close to 14 million people will see you."

Remy became intrigued. "Yeah?"

"And, Remy my boy, when you win the election, not if, you will be a household name and you won't have to spend your first months in Congress establishing your name!"

Remy shook his head in agreement. Hobbs had a point. "Okay, Walter. When?"

"She wants you to appear on Wednesday."

"Hobbs, that's the day after tomorrow!"

"Yes, I know. But the election is in two weeks!"

"Okay. I'm in."

The Opine people contacted Remy's people and prepared the segment. They asked Remy what he would like as his introduction music and where he would like to be seated near Wilma. The entire operation was first class he thought. Ms. Opine arranged for Remy's entire family to be flown out. In fact, he had such a comfortable feeling regarding Ms. Opine, that he was feeling confident about this appearance.

Remy chose "Psycho Therapy" as his intro music. Rachiel looked at her husband with Spock eyebrows, but Remy just smiled. After all, he had never had to choose theme music before.

The day arrived and Remy, Rachiel and the kids flew out to Manhattan. Opine's staff put Remy in the finest Hotel in Manhattan, and supplied them with tours of sights around Manhattan. Wilma was definitely proud of her city and she held back nothing to promote it. She instructed the tour guide to personally show the Gayos the historic areas in town.

Finally, in the mid-afternoon, they were taken to the television studio and Remy's family was seated in the front row of the audience.

"... And, on today's show, New York Congressional hopeful Remy Gayo!" Wilma announced enthusiastically to her audience.

A segment of the crowd cheered wildly while others just sat and stared ahead. Remy heard it and steeled himself. He knew that this would be a tough road ahead, in fact, maybe even hostile.

Remy took his seat and acknowledged the crowd after shaking the hand of Wilma, the Grande Dame of talk television.

"So, Remy. I appreciate you coming on today. I know it was short notice but your story has hit a chord with so many people out there!"

Remy leaned forward nervously in his chair. "I'm glad you brought that up Ms. Opine..."

"It's Wilma, Remy" as she flashed her million dollar smile at him.

"Wilma, thank you. However, I am rather curious. Not that I mind being a guest on your show!" The audience roared, even the ones who eyed him with suspicion.

Remy continued. "I mean, my campaign is for the 28th district of New York congressional seat and here I am in Manhattan. What makes me so interesting to be on your show?"

"Remy, thank you for the kind words. But, your story is so intriguing. After all, you're just a regular citizen with no background in politics. What did motivate you to run?"

"Wilma, I can go into the sordid details, but let's make this quick. Essentially I decided to stop feeling sorry for myself and complaining about things and decided to do something about it."

Wilma smiled. "About what Remy?"

"About the abandonment of the working class by the Federal government and what we just seem to accept from our elected officials. Wilma, we're being taken for granted. When we need the government's help, we get passed over, but... heaven forbid we forget to send in our tax payments!"

The crowd erupted into applause. Wilma smiled again and proceeded.

"So, do you think that you can make a difference?"

"Absolutely. Otherwise I wouldn't be in this."

Wilma smiled again. "Remy, I have to admit. Do you actually think that you have a chance? I mean, it's wonderful and all that you are the genuine article. But don't you think that your lack of experience will hinder you?"

"Wilma, I thought about that. Then I realized, yes. I can do it. My mother always told me that I can accomplish whatever I put my mind to. Isn't that what this country is all about? People who put their minds to problems and come up with solutions? And, after looking at what was actually in Washington I knew that I could do it. Besides, I think that we all forget that this country was built by people like me. Regular, working citizens!"

The crowd burst out in a large applause.

"It's great that you feel that way. I think we need more people to do what you're doing. After all, look at our President!"

The crowd clapped wildly at this, meantime Remy started laughing hard. Wilma looked at Remy, mildly chuckling to herself but curious at the outburst. "Remy, what's so funny?"

Remy composed himself. "Please, Wilma. You do yourself an injustice."

193

Wilma looked at him quizzically. "What, Remy? What injustice?"

"Wilma, honestly. Our President, like my opponent, they are far from being ordinary people. My opponent comes from an upper-middle class family, while our President, well, with all due respect and deference to his office, did not actually ever have to want for anything in his life."

Wilma became intrigued with this and kept silent as Remy continued. "Now, you, on the other hand, you are an amazing story. You built your career from the ground up and worked for everything you ever had."

Wilma smiled graciously. "Well, thank you."

"The President? Well, let's put it this way, Wilma, what was the name of the boarding school that you attended?"

Wilma looked at Remy with a smirk on her face. "Boarding school? Um, I didn't go to boarding school."

Remy smiled and continued. "Exactly, and when did you graduate from Harvard? Oh, that's right you didn't. You graduated from NYU, didn't you? Look, Wilma. You do yourself a disservice by trying to compare yourself to anyone else, especially a politician! You have built everything that you have on your own hard work and diligence. Even when you were given a scholarship, you took that and turned it into something more. Many of these people, all they do is live off of us. Our President? So he graduated from College, got a job in the community, then in congress, now as President. He has never earned his income on his own efforts. He has continually lived off of the work and income of others! Of us!"

The audience had a smattering of applause. Wilma stared at Remy, not with contempt, but with curiosity. She had never thought of it that way.

Remy smiled and decided to wrap it up. "Wilma, if anyone should run for President, it should be you!"

With that, the audience stood for a standing ovation. Wilma looked almost embarrassed. "Remy, thank you for the kind words. Now, back to my original question, what do you think your chances are?"

"Wilma, I can only do what I'm doing. Now, it's up to the American people. My opponent is a fine person herself, despite our differences of opinion on many matters. So, I say, as the system was originally set up, let the people decide."

Wilma cocked her head. "Remy, we have to wrap this up but, I have to ask. You never put down your opponents, not even when you don't agree with them. Don't you think that is going to hurt you?"

Remy closed his eyes in thought and answered. "Wilma, I used to get angry and defensive with the best of them. But, one thing my father taught me was that if you don't like someone just ignore them. If they start throwing sand at you while you're in the sandbox, move to a different area. Don't waste your energy on negative people. The truth will always prevail, even when you think it won't."

Wilma stood and clapped her hands towards Remy. "Amen to that, Remy. Good luck in the election. Everyone, let's thank Remy Gayo for coming on our show today!"

Wilma started to clap herself along with the audience. Rachiel and the children stood up to join the audience in a standing ovation. Remy smiled and shook Wilma's hand. The election was just around the corner.

Remy thought back on the campaign. Now it was up to the people to decide. Not the newspapers, television, pundits or prognosticators, no, it was up to the people. Remy would find out in a few days how well his message was received.

One thing was for sure. He didn't quit, and he's seeing through to its end.

As the excitement of the path he decided to pursue sunk in his thoughts went back to his father and grandfather. Is this what they would have wanted for him? Was this something that they would have done? Remy paused and cocked his head. Well, maybe not.

Maybe this wasn't what they would have done. But, one thing was for sure. They would have been proud of his new found efforts. He realized that before they had always doubted his work ethic, or maybe just thought that he didn't know how to apply it. And, rightfully so. He really didn't put enough effort into anything that he did. Things had been too easy to achieve without any concentrated effort from him. Now, however, forged by the fires of adversity, he realized his true mettle, his own work ethic.

Yes, he thought, his grandfather and father would be proud. For he finally found what they always had, the inner strength to be self-reliant man. He had become a man that could not only take care of himself, but, additionally, others. Win or lose, and he definitely began to think that he would win, this was it. Remy had finally realized that life wasn't about what it could give you, it was about what you could make of it, regardless of the obstacles it throws in front of you.

And, last, but not least, life was especially about the ability to nurture and raise your own kingdom, that is, your family, and to provide the basis, using your own strengths, a solid platform on which your own children can build and proceed on. Because, after all, isn't that what life is all about, Remy finally came to realize.

Definition of names:

Serafin: A variation on the word, Seraphim. These are the highest order of angel in the kingdom of God. The Seraphim have six wings and are the closest to God in terms of his purity and power.

Remiel: The "Mercy of God" archangel. A fallen watcher, he is also known as the angel of hope. In some translations he is the angel that watches over those that are to be resurrected.

Rachiel: A feminine variation of the name of the archangel Raguel. Raguel is the angel of justice, fairness, harmony, and vengeance.

Bruno: The name of Saint Bruno of Cologne. St. Bruno was a renown teacher and close advisor to Pope Urban II.

Regina: Latin variation of the word Queen.

Edward J. Indovina

About the Author

Edward J. Indovina has been reading stories for as long as he can remember.

As a young boy, his Mother and Father encouraged reading off all types which essentially led to his continuing love affair for comic books and all such graphic story telling.

As an offshoot of that he began a lifelong love affair with paperback pulp novels of all types.

Concurrently, Edward is the owner of one of the largest private collection of comic/pulp books to known man.

This is his first story based upon true historical events. In addition to this, he is the author of Adventures of John Hasard, currently printed by Pro Se Press, the soon to be published Children's book, "Melanie and the Easter Pig", and was the recent runner-up in the Buffalo Screams Horror script contest for his full length script entry, "Rosary". These are besides the many works currently in development.

The author currently lives in Rochester, NY with his wife-to-be, Dee and their son Sobe, an American Eskimo who has taken the place of their human children who have left the nest successfully.

Starry Night Books:

Your Stories

What Did I Do Wrong?
by Eveline Sandy

Teeta Heads West
by Bonnie West

The Dhikr of Authenticity
by Dawud Abdur-Rahman

A Women's Tool for Self-Empowerment
Organize Your Life for Success
365 Days of Empowerment Journal
by Dr. Perdita M. Meeks

Theft of a Nation
Treason
The CONstitution That Never Was
by Ralph Boryszewski

Vendetta
by Ed Frederico

Wonderings: Poems of Peace and Solace
by Rosemarie MacCheyene

My Dog Fluffy
by Andrew Stedmann

Pink Monkeys
The Adventures of Robin Caruso
Secrets to Writing Well
Marvin and Ted
Marvin! Marvin! Marvin!
Hurray For Marvin
Super-Marvin
by Richard S. Hartmetz

Murry Peterson Books:
Spy Game
Checkmate
Deceit
Failsafe
Iron Curtain
Echelon
The Final Countdown

Edward J. Indovina

OUR VISION

Our goal is to help you get your story into print. It really is that simple.

As authors ourselves, we understand the frustration of repeated rejections from the big publishing companies and the elitist agents. It becomes a Catch 22 when you have to be a big name in order to get published and become a big name. We're here to eliminate that step and the potential heartbreak that accompanies it and put the power back in your hands.

We are not a "vanity publisher" who charges you as much as $10,000 to receive a handful of substandard paperbacks, just so you can hand them out to the relatives at Christmas and never sell another copy. We get you published and marketed both in paperback and e-book format on Amazon.com and other major online retailers. We also don't charge to get you published, we only charge a small fee for preparing your book.

You earn up to a 60% royalty rate with us, instead of the typical 10% that the traditional publishing houses pay. Why should you do all the work and allow them to keep 90% of your profit? And the best part is, you retain 100% of the rights to your work!

THE FUTURE IS NOW!

Gone are the days when an author would sit in front of an old manual typewriter, rubbing holes in the paper or filling their office garbage cans with unsalvageable scrap. The publishing industry is evolving. The old publishing houses are becoming dinosaurs. E-books are everywhere. They are cheaper than old-fashioned books, use less paper and ink, faster to produce, take up less space and can be read on any computer, e-reader or Smartphone.

Success comes to those who make opportunities happen, not those who wait for opportunities to happen. You can be successful too, you just have to try...

A recent poll suggested that nearly 85% of parents would encourage their child to read a book on an e-reader. More than 1 in 5 of us owns an e-reading device and the number is climbing rapidly. For every 100 hardcover books that Amazon sells, it sells 143 e-books. They also never go out of print!

Hundreds of thousands of independent authors, just like you, are selling their profitable work as you read this. E-book sales have grown over 200% in the past year and account for more than $1 billion in annual sales.

Chances are, you don't even know the difference between a PDF, mobi, ePub, doc, azw, or the fifteen other competing formats struggling to coexist on the sixteen types of e-reader devices such as the Kindle or the Nook. Even if you are able to keep up with all the devices and their formats, do you want to spend the money for expensive software to convert your files, or the many hours it will take to figure out how it works? Will you be able to create an interactive table of contents?

Our editors are professionals with experience in computer science, graphic design and publishing. We can do the work or you, creating a top-notch book that you will be proud of. Of course, you still have to write it, but that's the fun part...

BE A PART OF OUR COMMUNITY

Reach your intended audience in the worldwide marketplace by distributing your work on Amazon, Barnes and Noble and other major online booksellers. Earn royalties, get feedback, Join the discussions in the forum and meet other people in our community who share the same interests you do.

We will publish your fiction or non-fiction books about just about anything, including poetry, education, gardening, health, history, humor, law, medicine, pets, philosophy, political science, psychology, music, science, self-help travel, science-fiction, fantasy, mystery, thriller, children and young adult, etc....

http://www.starrynightpublishing.com

CPSIA information can be obtained at www.ICGtesting.com
Printed in the USA
BVOW030958130513

320571BV00012B/174/P